Tally the Witch

The Books of Fatebane

———— ● ————

Tally the Witch

Book One of Fatebane

Molly Landgraff

ISBN-10 1549671294
ISBN-13 978-1549671296

Published by Molly Landgraff.
Cover art by Matthew Lind.

Set in Libre Caslon Text
and Merriweather
by Rose Davidson.

To Amy and Jane

The Choosing

I never actually set out to become a witch. When I snuck into the witches' wagon during the Choosing, it was to steal the herbs I needed to make the medicine that would help my sister. Shalla had been sick for some time now, with the same wasting sickness that had claimed our parents, along with most of the village we had lived in, earlier that year. Uncle Grim took us in, but he was not a wealthy man and medicines were expensive, so I had to stretch out the supply of dried herbs I'd claimed from the old herbalist's shop before we came to Tancred's Ford to live with him. The Choosing was the first opportunity I'd seen to replenish my supply, and seemed like a sure bet.

The Choosing happens every year in autumn. The Great Coven, the grand assembly of all the witches in the land, assembles twice a year, in spring and autumn. In their autumn assembly, any apprentice who is able to pass the trials is allowed to graduate and become a full-fledged witch, and those new witches are sent out shortly after to choose their own apprentices. This year, three such new witches had sent word to Tancred's Ford that they would be seeking hopeful apprentices there. Nearly every girl in town between the ages of twelve and fourteen had gathered for the occasion, hoping to be chosen to become an apprentice witch. It was an honour to be selected, and would be a boon to the region once the girls graduated, if any chose to come back and serve the town as the resident witch. Given that there was no witch currently in residence in the area, I suspected that the Choosing was taking place here partly for that reason as well.

I had ducked out of the house early that morning, avoiding Uncle Grim and his chores. He had a hard time understanding me, I knew—he thought a young boy should be eager to grow into a strapping young man, and didn't understand that I didn't feel that at all. I spent more time with books and stories than I did with the other boys in town, and enjoyed sharing romantic tales with Shalla, who was often too sick to read herself. Uncle Grim wasn't the only one who didn't understand, either. I had avoided the other boys since my early days in Tancred's Ford, when I had returned home with a blackened eye and bruises from where they had beaten me, which they called 'initiating the new kid.' I didn't want anything to do with them after that. Who would? Occasionally they still threw stones at me as I passed, but otherwise they ignored me.

The Choosing had begun early, with all the hopeful girls lined up. There were three witches, as advertised. The first was tall and beautiful, like an enchantress from a storybook, but her beauty was severe and more than a little cold. The second was short and round, and wore a warm and cheerful smile, and seemed quite motherly. The third witch was of average height, and wore half-moon spectacles. With her hair pulled into a tight bun, she reminded me of nothing so much as a librarian. None of them were paying attention as I slipped into the back of the wagon and began rummaging around. I'd managed to find a small chest filled with glass jars of herbs and was rifling through it looking for the ones I'd need, when from behind me came a wry voice.

"You know, most people are too put off by the prospect of being turned into a newt or put under a curse unto the seventh generation to try to steal from witches," said the woman—obviously a witch, from her black dress and manner—as she stepped up into the back of the wagon and blocked my escape. "You're a brave little one, aren't you?" She crouched and plucked the jars of herbs from my unresisting hands, examining them. "Brave and smart," she mused. "You're not just picking these out randomly, are you?"

I shook my head mutely. She looked at them again, and frowned. "What else were you looking for?" she demanded in a sharper tone.

"St Tobias' Wort," I mumbled, "and feverfew."

The witch nodded thoughtfully. "Medicine for the wasting sickness? You've mixed these before?" she asked. I nodded in return. "Show me," she said, pointing to a small bench where I could work.

Nervously, I set to work, as though mixing the concoction for Shalla, with the witch watching silently over my shoulder. When I was done mixing the herbs in the required proportions, I turned and spoke apologetically.

"It needs to brew over a fire," I said, "like a tea, but for longer."

"Who do you make it for?" asked the witch gently.

I saw little reason to lie at this point, and since she had not cursed me or turned me into a newt, I hesitated only a moment before answering.

"My sister, Shalla," I admitted, then added "She's very sick."

"Indeed," said the witch. "Come, take me to her." She rose and climbed out of the wagon, beckoning to me to follow.

Outside, two other witches were still inspecting the girls and asking them questions. The tall and beautiful witch stood by with Constance Tailor, who was looking insufferably smug. "Wait a moment," said the witch with me, and she strode over to the witch standing with Constance and, gesturing to me, apparently explained the situation. The other witch's expression went from nonplussed to downright displeased, but in the end she nodded.

The witch who had caught me was the youngest of the group of witches, though still obviously old enough to be considered an adult, and there was a slight air of mischief to her that I now noticed—a crooked grin as she returned to me and nodded.

"Right," she said, "let's go visit your sister. My name is Rosaleth," she added. "How are you called?"

"My name is Tal," I answered, confused a bit by her phrasing.

"Ah," she replied, silent for a time. It did not take us long to get back to Uncle Grim's smithy, where Uncle Grim was working the forge. He paused to stare briefly at the witch and I as we approached. He raised no objection, though—he likely hoped, as I secretly hoped, that this Rosaleth might be able to do more than just ease Shalla's pain. I nodded to him casually, as if showing up with a witch in tow was an everyday occurrence. He raised an eyebrow, but nodded back, and went back to his work.

Inside, the curtains were drawn. "Shalla?" I called softly, moving to open them slightly, if only to give some of the stale air passage to the cool autumn day and bring some freshness to the house. "Shalla, I've brought someone to visit. She's a witch, named Rosaleth."

Shalla sat up weakly in bed, reading. She looked over, pale and beautiful, and smiled shyly. "Hullo," she said quietly. "I hope Tal didn't bother you too much to get you to come look at me," she continued.

Rosaleth smiled wryly and shook her head. "Tal was just showing me how he makes your medicine," she said, "and wanted to know if there was anything he could do better."

Taking the cue, I put the mixed herbs I'd prepared in the wagon into the kettle to boil. Rosaleth chatted softly with Shalla as I worked, asking her questions about the book she was reading, the town, and a couple about our parents, our uncle, and me.

"Oh, Uncle Grim is very good to us, to have taken us in," Shalla said, "but I wish he understood Tal is a gentle soul, and doesn't fit in well with the other boys and their rough games." I felt my cheeks reddening and turned, pouring a cup of the concoction I'd mixed for Shalla.

"Here, now," I said, "there's no need for that. Drink up," I added, passing her the cup. Looking relieved, Shalla drank, then coughed again. I looked at Rosaleth, to see what her reaction would be, and found her looking back at me, an odd expression on her face.

"Well done," was all she said.

Rosaleth suggested that Shalla should rest, and Shalla agreed easily, so we bade her farewell—Rosaleth, it seemed, was not finished with me yet, as she crooked a finger to indicate I should accompany her. Outside, we walked silently for a few moments, then she broke the silence with a question.

"Would you like to be a witch, Tal?"

I stopped walking. "I—I can't," I stammered. "Boys can't be witches, everyone knows that."

"I didn't ask that," she said, cocking her eyebrow at me. "I asked if you'd like to be a witch."

I looked down, feeling heat in my cheeks, in my belly, and did not reply for a moment.

"Yes, I would," I said finally.

"Are you willing to follow my instructions, even if you don't understand them?" she asked. I nodded.

"Are you willing to leave your home, and trust your sister's care to your Uncle?" she asked. I hesitated, and she added, "who will be supplied with the medicine she needs, of course." I nodded again, then.

"Are you willing to be an outcast, never truly welcome among the people you help?" she asked, with a hint of bitterness.

"I'm already an outcast," I said. "I'm the weird boy, and..."

"From now on, you're the weird *girl*," Rosaleth corrected. "If you become my apprentice, that is. It will be hard work, but I think you'll do well.Will you accept?"

The feeling in my chest was confusing. Rosaleth was offering me a way to stop stealing herbs to save my sister, and more—she was offering me training in herbs, in healing, and in *magic.* And...she'd identified, somehow, my innermost secret, and was offering me a way to be who I'd always wanted to be, but never known of a way to become.

"Yes," I said. "Yes I will."

"Then come on," Rosaleth said, satisfied. "Let's go introduce you to your fellow apprentices. And get you into some proper clothes. I can't have my apprentice dressing like a boy, now can I?"

I grinned back at her and shook my head.

My Fellow Apprentices

Rosaleth and I returned to the witches wagon. "We'll have clothes that you can wear," she told me, "at least for now. They won't fit perfectly, but they'll probably do."

"What about...you know," I asked, blushing. "Will you just magic me into a girl?"

Rosaleth shook her head, a little sadly. "It doesn't work that way, I'm afraid," she said. "Once, the most powerful witches could transform entire kingdoms, but these days it takes the Grand Coven all working together to perform that kind of magic." Seeing my face fall, she added, "It doesn't mean we won't be able to change you, just not instantly. It takes a lot of magic to change people, but we can get your body to do a lot of the work before..."

I felt lost in her explanation, and it clearly showed on my face. She sighed.

"It's easier to change someone into something close to what they already are. I couldn't make your Uncle Grim into a woman, not without a lot of magic and a lot of help. He's just not made that way. You're not your Uncle Grim, Tally," she said, seeing my dismay. "You're already part of the way there, up here." She tapped my temple gently. "With the right mixture of ingredients, I'll be able to make you a potion. It'll likely taste awful, and you'll have to drink it every day, but it'll make your body grow like a girl's body, instead of a boy's body. Do you understand?"

I nodded slowly. "So...once I've become more like a girl in body and not just in my mind, you'll be able to use magic easier to change me all the way?" I asked, then paused. "Also...Tally?"

Rosaleth nodded, grinning impishly. "You got it. It's cute, don't you think?"

I just blushed.

The dresses Rosaleth produced from in a large chest tucked

away in the wagon were clearly hand-me-downs, presumably—given that they were all black—from other young witches. She was right that they didn't fit perfectly, but one of them seemed to more or less suit my frame in a not-unflattering way. I emerged from the wagon to find her in hushed but heated discussion with the other witches—the tall, beautiful one seemed to be angry with her for some reason.

It quickly became apparent that reason was me.

"I thought you weren't choosing an apprentice," said the tall witch. "Now you come back and tell us that you've not only chosen, but that your apprentice is—" She broke off, seeing me.

"I changed my mind," Rosaleth said calmly. "She impressed me." Rosaleth laid no particular emphasis on the word, but I felt a thrill at being called "she" all the same.

"It's neither unprecedented nor all that troublesome, Evie," the plump witch said, trying to smooth the situation over. "Besides, it's Rosaleth's right to choose her own apprentice as she will."

"Be that as it may, Alina" said the stern-looking witch I had thought of as looking like a librarian earlier, as she regarded me over her half-moon spectacles. "You can't deny that we sent word saying we would be choosing three apprentices from this town, not four. These people can count to four, and we'll be hearing about the boy we ensorcelled for years."

"I'm not a boy," I said angrily "and I haven't been ensorcelled." I realized I had spoken out of turn almost immediately. The librarian-witch gave me a look as if she had discovered half a worm in her apple, and I was it.

"You will speak when spoken to, girl, and you will refer to your elders with respect," she said coldly. "I am Mistress Lirella. This is Mistress Eve and Mistress Alina. I take it Mistress Rosaleth has not instructed you on proper etiquette," she continued with a glare at Rosaleth—*Mistress* Rosaleth.

"Hadn't got to that yet," Mistress Rosaleth said.

"I shall leave it to you to educate your apprentice as you will, as is your right Mistress Rosaleth, but if she speaks out of turn again or shows me such disrespect again I shall punish her as is *my* right." She turned to me, her expression still stern, but not unkind. "You are correct, young lady, that you are not a boy—but there will be whispers all the same from those who do not know better. I welcome you to the sisterhood of witches."

"That's you outvoted, Evie." Mistress Alina smiled. "Welcome, child—what is your name?"

"Tally, Mistress Alina," I said.

Mistress Alina laughed, a warm sound. "You learn quickly, young Tally. Don't worry, I won't be angry if you forget to say mistress—it always makes me feel old." She winked. "You'll soon learn that no two witches are quite the same. A good thing, by all accounts."

Rosaleth cleared her throat. "I was just going to send Tally to join her fellow chosen, before the feast,' she said. "We can finish our discussion later, ladies—we have work to do now."

Mistress Eve did not look pleased to be overruled by her colleagues, and doubly so to be put off so expertly, but she raised no further objection. Rosaleth pointed me to an area off near the wagon, where three other girls—already outfitted in black, I saw—sat chatting quietly to one another.

"Hullo," I greeted the other girls as I drew near. Constance glanced up at me and wrinkled her face in an expression of distaste. I knew she was one of the chosen—she'd been chosen before Rosaleth whisked me off, after all—but did not know much else about her. She had long, brown hair, worn in fancy braids. It made me slightly self-conscious of my own short, messy hair.

"I thought there were to be *three* of us," Constance said, her tone unfriendly. "Why are you here?"

I sighed inwardly. "Mistress Rosaleth chose me," I said, cheerfully, ignoring Constance's venomous glare. "She hadn't planned to choose an apprentice, but I must have impressed her."

"That's wonderful!" the second of the three girls said, clapping. It took me a moment to place her—the baker's daughter, I thought. She was a plump girl, with blonde hair framing her face, but energetic and enthusiastic. "I'm Silke," she continued. "Mistress Alina chose me! I don't think I know you, though," she added in a tone of slight confusion.

"That's Tal," said the third girl, quietly—by process of elimination, Mistress Lirella's apprentice. I knew her, too—Sara, the bookseller's daughter. She had dark skin, and wore her hair long and loose.It made sense that she would be chosen—there wasn't anyone smarter in town. We'd been acquaintances almost as long as I could recall, since I'd frequented the bookseller's shop often, both to get new stories for Shalla to read and to get new books on herbs to try and cure her.

"Tally," I corrected. "I'm Tally." Sara raised an eyebrow, but nodded. It seemed she grasped the situation immediately, and I was suddenly glad to have found a friend so quickly.

"Tally," she said. "She's the blacksmith's niece—you probably never saw her because she's been taking care of her sister."

The confusion on Silke's face cleared instantly. "That makes perfect sense!" she said. "You must know a lot about healing, then—I've heard that...well I heard that your sister is very sick."

"She is," I said quietly. "I do what I can, but—"

"I'm sorry," Constance interrupted me, "but before we were interrupted, we had just agreed that I would have my father make us all new dresses. He's the best tailor in miles, you know, and these hand-me-downs just will not do. It won't cost us a thing, either, of course, since my father loves me so much. I'm sure he won't mind helping my new friends, either."

Silke, Sara, and I exchanged glances. Silke shrugged. "I'm all right with these," she said. "Dresses are expensive, even if your father would make them without asking for money, and this fits well enough for now—"

"There's no such thing as 'well enough'," Constance said. "We're witches now, or apprentices—we're better than those who weren't chosen. Well..." she said, eyeing me, "Most of us are. Regardless, I shall speak to father after the feast—"

"Yeah, about this feast," I interrupted, "I'm not sure what that's about. I just heard about it now from Rosaleth—Mistress Rosaleth, I mean—but I don't know anything more about it."

Constance's glare could have melted iron, but Silke piped up.

"It's a farewell feast for us," she said. "Our families are invited to bid us goodbye, since we'll be gone for a long time—years perhaps, between visits."

I swallowed, thinking of Shalla. "Our families..." Then I realized that I would have to explain this to Uncle Grim, too—all of it.

That was a far less pleasant prospect than facing down a thousand of Constance's glares in the days to come.

The Feast

Of course Rosaleth didn't give me a chance to explain before the feast. Before long a table had been brought out from somewhere and laden with food, which the witches were bringing out from the wagon.

"That smells delicious," said Silke, gazing at the various dishes longingly.

"Where is it coming from?" I asked. The others turned to look at me. "I mean, I was inside that wagon, there's no oven or stove or larder in there that I saw..."

"Obviously it's magic," said Constance airily. "Are you really sure you're supposed to be here?"

Before I could reply, Sara interrupted. "You were inside the wagon?" she asked quietly. I nodded, realizing that further discussion of precisely what I was doing there may not be the wisest thing to admit, even to my fellow apprentices.

"Well aren't you special," Constance said, a sneer on her face. "Getting to be the fourth out of three girls chosen, getting to see inside the wagon when the rest of us haven't."

"I didn't say that," I said. "I just said—"

"You didn't have to say it. I didn't even see you lined up with the rest of us. You probably bribed your mistress somehow to take you on, instead of letting some other girl more worthy have your spot."

"I did nothing of the sort," I said. "I never asked to be picked, but what was I supposed to do, say no? I—" I stopped, flush with anger. This wasn't helping anything.

"Yes," Constance said, turning up her nose at me.

"That's enough," Silke said. "There's no need to be so rude, Constance. You were chosen first, before anyone else, don't you think that's enough?"

I stalked away before Constance could reply, suddenly not wanting to hear any more from her. Sara followed after me. I stopped, not willing to go too far.

"She's jealous," Sara said quietly. "Before you, she was the special one, from being picked first. Now it's you who's the special one."

"I never asked to be special," I said, knowing how childish I sounded.

"But you are special, Tally. I'm curious about that, by the way— you being Tally, I mean, instead of Tal. How long...?"

"Always," I said, glad for a change of topic, even to this. "I've always known, but there was never anything I could do about it so..." I trailed off, shrugging. I'd found myself wishing, often enough, when I was alone at night, that I could be the person I knew inside that I should be, but it had never been something I could act on.

Sara nodded, her expression thoughtful. "I won't say anything to anyone, until you tell me otherwise" she promised.

I suddenly felt the urge to hug her. "You're a good friend," I told her. "I don't know what I'm going to do about my Uncle. I think Shalla will be fine with it, though."

"There's only one thing to do," she said after a moment's thought. "He may not understand the truth, or even accept it, but if you don't tell him the truth about this then..." Sara trailed off.

"I know." I groaned. "Mistress Lirella was saying the same thing, people might claim I've been ensorcelled and stolen away." If people noticed at all that I was gone, that is. I didn't exactly have many friends in Tancred's Ford, and the one person I would count as a friend outside of my family was coming, too.

Sara nodded, her expression serious. "She's right, of course. People would talk—they already will. If your Uncle knows the truth, he can put those sorts of rumours to bed."

I sighed. "What am I going to do about Constance?" I asked. "She doesn't even know me, and she already seems to hate me."

Sara smiled at me, and I saw a hint of ferocity in that smile. "You'll just have to be better than she is," she said. "I know you can do it. Here," she added, handing me a handkerchief. "Dry your eyes—I see our families coming."

I rubbed at my face, surprised to see I'd been crying—when had *that* happened?—and followed Sara back towards the others.

Thankfully it seemed that Constance and Silke were already

moving to join their families for a short bit of time in private, to say goodbye before the big official feast in front of everyone. Constance's parents looked very proud of her, and her mother seemed to be crying a little as well—I felt sudden sympathy in spite of myself, as I saw Constance struggling not to cry herself. She seemed to be very close to her family, and I wondered if she was lashing out at me because she was stressed out over being separated from them.Silke's parents just looked very happy for her, and Sara's family looked as calm and collected as ever.

As for my family, Uncle Grim looked at me with some confusion and a questioning expression, as he approached slowly, supporting Shalla gently on his arm. Shalla was all smiles, which gave me hope. I approached to help.

"So I have a little sister now," Shalla said as I took her other arm. "Rosaleth told us to call you Tally now. It's a cute name," she added.

"Ah, yeah," was all I managed. I looked at Uncle Grim, but his expression was, as always, serious.

"So," he said.

"So," I answered. We stood together, the three of us, for a few moments.

"This...is this what you truly want?" Uncle Grim asked finally. "Being a witch? Being a girl?"

"It is," I said, nodding firmly. I swallowed hard. "I...never knew how to say before, but it's how I've always felt."

"I can't say I understand it fully," Uncle Grim said slowly, "but I want you to know that you'll still have a place here if you need one. Tal or Tally, you're my family. I don't think I need to understand to support you in this."

"What he means," Shalla said, "is that we love you just the same as always no matter what." She coughed softly.

"Is the medicine still working? Will you be okay?" I asked, worried for her.

"I'll be fine," she said. "Rosaleth said she'll help me back home if I need to leave early, so that you can spend more time with Uncle Grim before you go as well."

"I'm glad you came," I said. I gave them both big hugs. "I didn't know if I would get a chance to say goodbye."

Shalla reached out and ruffled my hair. "You'll have to write often, of course, little Tally," she said. "Or we'll think you don't love us anymore."

"I'll always love you," I said, and meant it. "I'll write as often as I can. I swear."

"Now now," Uncle Grim said, a bit embarrassed at the extended hug. He was never very good with feelings. "Look, they're ready for us. Let's go eat."

In truth I don't recall much about the specifics of the feast. I remember Rosaleth winking at me as I approached the table with Uncle Grim and Shalla. I remember that Constance, like everyone else, was too overwhelmed at saying goodbye to her family to be particularly snappish at me. I remember that the food was delicious, and no matter how much we ate, there always seemed to be seconds or thirds available. I remember Shalla, looking healthier than she had in a long time, staying almost to the end of the evening, and Rosaleth winking at me as she went to help Shalla back home when she became too tired to stay any longer.

Most of all I remember everyone's faces, and the pride they showed for their daughters. Uncle Grim, too, looked proud of me, in a way he never had when he'd thought I was a very bookish boy—and I knew that it was true, that even if he never understood how I felt, he would always be there for me if I needed support at all, and that no matter what happened I would always have a home here in Tancred's Ford.

After the feast, we new apprentices stood with our mistresses as our families bade us a final goodbye.

"I'm sure Shalla will be waiting for your letters," Uncle Grim said gruffly. "So remember your promise."

"I will," I said, holding back my tears as best I could.

"I'm proud of you, Tally," he said, clasping my shoulder. "I always knew you were more than ordinary, and this just shows it's true. You remember that—you're special." He squeezed my shoulder once, and then turned to Rosaleth.

"I'll take good care of her," she said. "I'll send fresh herbs around regularly for Shalla, too. You'll see improvement as long as the herbs are fresh, and she takes them every day. By this time next year, she may not need them anymore."

I blinked. "You mean she wasn't getting better because of the age of the herbs?" I asked, surprised.

Rosaleth nodded. "They were losing potency the longer you held onto them—and I'm willing to bet you were using less when you could for fear of running out."

Uncle Grim's face broke into a smile—an unfamiliar expression on his normally somber face. "It'll be good to see her well, won't it, Tally? When you visit next, I bet she'll have a million stories for you, too."

I couldn't hold back any longer, and I burst into tears. "Thank you," I said, hugging Rosaleth impulsively. "Thank you so much."

"Hey now," Rosaleth said, a little awkwardly. "I'm going to work you hard, Tally, so don't thank me just yet." She took my hand. "Now...are you ready to take the first steps on your journey to becoming a true witch?"

I nodded, smiling through my tears. "Of course!"

The Wagon

Rosaleth brought me back to join the others—each girl standing now with her mistress.

"Time to clean up." Rosaleth sighed. Mistress Alina seemed to be the only one cheerful about that prospect—Mistress Eve and Mistress Lirella both looked as nonplussed as Rosaleth at the prospect of cleaning up the remnants of the feast.

"Clean-up is part of the job," Mistress Alina said in a cheery voice. "Come on, ladies, the sooner we finish the sooner we'll be done."

"That's tautological, but not especially motivational," said Mistress Lirella. "Girls, please stand aside for now. Tonight, we'll handle the cleanup, but do not expect to be waited on from here on out. Your training begins in earnest tomorrow."

Constance seemed all to happy to take charge of us apprentices. I didn't protest, since I was busy focusing on what the witches were doing. Mistress Alina had her sleeves rolled up and was busy scrubbing dishes, with Mistress Lirella drying. Rosaleth and Eve were working together to lift the big table back onto the wagon, and it seemed they were arguing with each other while they did so. From a snippet I overheard, I thought I might be the subject of their debate—but before I could move closer to try and eavesdrop, Constance grabbed my shoulder.

"I asked you a question, Tally," she said. "It's very rude of you not to be paying attention when your seniors are speaking to you."

"Senior? By what, an hour at most? Don't be ridiculous," I said, irritated. "I'm not going to bow and scrape to you just because of that, Constance, so you can forget it."

"Please don't fight," Silke said, grimacing. "There's no need for us to argue."

I sighed. "What were you asking me, Constance?" I asked.

"I asked," she replied airily, "if you knew why Mistress Rosaleth chose you. I'll accept that you didn't engage in any sort of trickery or underhanded methods, and yes, I'm sorry for suggesting that earlier," she said, her tone devoid of anything resembling remorse, "but you must know something about why you were selected to become her apprentice."

"I honestly don't," I said guardedly. "I was...asking for some herbs to help my sister Shalla—"

"The sick girl, yes? She at least seemed to have proper manners," Constance said, interrupting me. I ground my teeth, but I could see Sara behind Constance shaking her head, so rather than another retort, I simply continued.

"Yes, she's very sick. And since I already knew what herbs I'd need, Rosaleth—"

"Mistress Rosaleth," Constance said, looking unimpressed with me for forgetting the title.

"*Mistress* Rosaleth," I said, "asked me to show her how I would prepare the herbs into a tisane for Shalla. I guess i impressed her."

"Nonsense," Constance said immediately. "It's clear now— you're a charity case."

"Actually, Constance" Silke said, "I think it makes sense that—"

"Since you're a charity case," Constance continued, cutting Silke off, "I expect you'll stand aside and let the rest of us learn without holding us back."

"And just why would Tally hold you back, Constance?" Sara asked. "We've none of us learned anything yet about witchcraft, but Tally is already an accomplished herbalist—to some extent," she amended. "Do you know anything about herbs? I certainly don't."

"I know about spices," Silke said, a bit wounded. "And mixing and following recipes."

"You'll probably do well, then," I told her. "Mostly I just followed the instructions in the books, but...there were definitely things I didn't understand well." Like potency, I thought.

"We'll see." Constance sniffed. "I still expect that you'll offer respect and deference to the rest of us—"

"Where you've earned none," Mistress Lirella said, approaching us—it seemed she had finished with the dishes while we were bickering. "I warn you, young Constance—you're a clever girl with a great deal of potential, which is why you were chosen, but you should always remember that you are not the only clever girl with a great deal of potential. All of you are equals, and I for one expect each of you to behave with that in mind. I'm sure my sisters will agree. We have finished cleaning up—it is time to retire for the night. Please, join us inside the wagon."

I nearly protested that there was no way that the wagon would fit all eight of us, but I remembered the look I'd got from Mistress Lirella earlier—and I remembered too that I had not seen any sign of the table or other furnishings when I was inside it earlier, nor the food. The last thing I needed right now, too, was to give Constance further excuses to mock me, as—loath as I was to admit it—she'd probably been right earlier about the wagon being magical.

The wagon, I amended as I climbed inside, was definitely magical. It also looked nothing like the inside of the dim, somewhat pungent smelling wagon I had snuck into earlier today—instead, I would swear it was now larger inside than outside, and held a cheery wood stove burning in a corner, filling the air with the pleasant scent of wood smoke. Eight bedrolls were laid out on the floor nearby.

"Welcome, girls," said Mistress Eve solemnly, "to the Witches' Wagon. For the next few days this will be your home, while we travel to our permanent residences. Each of us has been assigned a cottage, and a village to care for, and you will dwell with your mistress there until such time as you become full witches yourselves. This wagon is, obviously, magical—you will say nothing to anyone else to that effect. This is the living chamber."

"It beats sleeping on the ground," Rosaleth said, winking at me as she spoke.

"Indeed," Mistress Eve said, giving her a slightly dirty look. "And you girls will ensure that that remains true. There are other chambers in the wagon, but unless we need them for some reason we will keep to this one. You girls will be in charge of sweeping the dirt and dust out every day and keeping it clean."

"Silke, you and I will manage the cooking," Mistress Alina said, "so you don't have to worry about sweeping—if that is agreeable to everyone, of course."

Mistress Eve nodded. It had seemed like she was in charge of the witches, at least as much as any of them were—though I could already tell that the others largely did what they wanted regardless of Mistress Eve's opinion. That dynamic seemed pretty familiar already—it was matched by Constance's behaviour towards the rest of us apprentices.

"We'll be travelling for a few days," Mistress Lirella said. "Along the way we'll be stopping for lessons where appropriate. For the time being, you will treat an instruction from any of us as though it came from your own mistress. Obviously this will change once we have arrived at our permanent residences, but for now I expect obedience from all of you, regardless of which of us issues you a task."

That seemed fair enough, too. Mistress Lirella seemed to be the sensible sort, if somewhat stern, and I could see why she'd pick Sara of all the girls in town—they had a collectedness and coolness about them in common that spoke of competence and quiet sensibility.

Now that I thought about it, too, Mistress Alina and Silke were an obvious match—both of them clearly enjoyed preparing food, and were already quietly discussing meal plans for tomorrow. Constance and Mistress Eve were also a perfect match, of course—they were both somewhat haughty. Or in Constance's case, very haughty, I amended.

I glanced at Rosaleth. She winked at me, grinning. If all of us were matched well to our witches, what did that say about me? What kind of person was Rosaleth? She seemed nice, but she also had not planned to take an apprentice at all—and I didn't really think it was just my amateur herbalism, barely a novice level, that had truly caught her eye. Was I really a charity case? I resolved to ask her, privately of course, about it, at the first opportunity.

"Tomorrow afternoon," Mistress Eve said, "we shall begin by teaching you how to summon and master your very own familiars."

"What's a familiar?" Silke asked. I was glad of that—it saved me having to be the one to inquire. From Constance's reaction, though, I probably wouldn't have needed to worry, as she seemed just as lost as Silke and I.

"A familiar is an animal companion and assistant," Sara offered, "who helps a witch in many ways. I read about them once."

"Do you all have familiars?" Constance asked, looking around. "I don't see any animals—"

"We don't keep them in the wagon with us. Helps keep things clean. And a lot less sarcastic," Rosaleth told her. "You'll meet our familiars tomorrow. Almost every witch has one. It's generally one of the first things that new apprentices learn, for a few reasons. We'll get into that tomorrow. It's going to be a big day, so you should get some rest now, girls."

The other witches seemed to agree on that point, at least, so we all climbed into the bedrolls and soon enough the sounds of breathing grew regular and even. I found myself unable to fall asleep easily, though, kept awake by trying to sort out the whirlwind of the day's events, and by the worry nagging at the back of my mind that Constance may be right—that I may be a charity case.

Eventually, though, even that drifted away, and I too fell into slumber.

Familiar

The next morning I awoke to the pleasant smell of frying bacon. I sat up, rubbing my eyes blearily.

"Thought you might sleep all day," Rosaleth said from nearby, grinning. "I told them to let you sleep in a little bit. Eve and Lirella didn't like it much but you're my apprentice so they couldn't really argue."

I grunted something resembling human speech. Rosaleth just smiled.

"Did I sleep in that long?" I yawned, stretching.

"Not really," Rosaleth said. "Actually, I was coming in to wake you for breakfast. I'm sure you'll want to go wash up first—be quick about it, all right?"

By the time I got back from washing up, a plate of bacon and eggs was waiting for me, with a side of spiced potatoes. It smelled heavenly. Silke beamed at me as I took a moment to enjoy the smell before tucking in.

"The potatoes are my special recipe," she said proudly. "Passed down from my mother."

"They're delicious," I said, after swallowing my first mouthful. "Thank you."

Silke continued to beam, and I decided I liked her. She seemed to frequently side with Constance, or at least, not side against her, but she was a friendly and cheerful person in general and if nothing else didn't seem to share Constance's prejudices.

Speaking of which, of course, Constance was already looking for ways to make my life more difficult, I was certain. Sure enough, as I glanced over at her, she smiled at me.

"Since you slept in, I say it's only fair that you get to clean up the dishes, Tally," she said, smiling cruelly. "We all had to help get ready, after all, while you got to sleep as long as you liked."

I didn't bother to protest. It didn't feel like it would do any good, and I had the feeling that if Constance was felt to be out of line by any of the witches, they would speak up like Mistress Lirella had last night, but none of them were, not even Rosaleth. I just sighed, and nodded, and kept working on my breakfast. It really was delicious.

"I'll help with that," Sara said. "She shouldn't have to do it alone, even if she did sleep in." I felt a surge of gratitude towards her. There, I was sure, I had a true friend.

"I'll wash," I said, "and you dry?" She nodded her assent.

It wasn't that bad to clean up in the end, with Sara's help. It went quick enough that we were soon on the road, moving at a brisk pace. We ate a lunch of sandwiches without stopping (also delicious—Silke and Mistress Alina certainly knew their craft,) and to my mind, made a good distance before finally stopping in the late afternoon.

"All right, girls," Mistress Lirella said briskly as we climbed out of the wagon. "It's time for you to learn about familiars."

Silke clapped excitedly, Constance looked eager, and even Sara smiled, her white teeth standing out against her dark skin. I had to admit, I was a little excited myself.

Okay, more than a little. From the sounds of things, a familiar was like a pet, but a very special pet, a magical pet that could also be your friend and partner. I'd never had a pet, and only a few friends, so there was definitely an appeal here.

The four witches lined up, and each closed their eyes and concentrated. A snowy owl glided silently from the forest and landed on Mistress Eve's shoulder. A large frog hopped forward from the underbrush, and Mistress Alina leaned down and scooped him up in both hands. A cat, black-furred—of course—was rubbing against Mistress Lirella's legs, having sauntered out from behind her as though it was the greatest trick ever performed, and for Rosaleth, a weasel streaked out and she laughingly scooped it up in her arms.

"These are our familiars," Mistress Eve said. Her owl extended its wings slightly and dipped forward, almost as if to bow.

"At your service," an elegant female voice sounded in my mind. I glanced around and saw the other girls looking confused as well as to the source of the voice.

"Are new witches always so slow?" asked another voice, deep and masculine, as Mistress Lirella's cat stalked forward and in-

spected us. *"You would think they had not been expecting anything at all."*

"They can talk!" Silke exclaimed delightedly.

"Of course we can, dearie" a new voice—I thought it was Mistress Alina's frog—said. *"We wouldn't be much use at all if we couldn't at least do that much."*

"Most familiars tend to be a little sarcastic," Rosaleth said. "Nobody's sure why."

"A little sarcastic? You wound me, mistress. I am extremely sarcastic" sounded a fourth voice in our minds, obviously Rosaleth's familiar.

"Shh," she chided him. "This is Snickers," she said by way of introduction. "And there is Midnight, Miss Geraldine, and Lady Snow," she said, indicating in turn the cat, the frog, and the owl.

"Notice," said Snickers, *"that as Rosaleth's familiar, I am the only one named without any thought to my inherent dignity and poise. Snickers indeed."*

"I've always found it eminently suited to you," Midnight the cat said.

Mistress Lirella cleared her throat. The comments from the assorted familiars quieted.

"Today, you'll begin your training as witches by calling your very own familiars, for which we will need to show you how to use your second sight." she told us. "Sara, please come here." As Sara stepped forward, the other witches likewise beckoned to us to join them.

Rosaleth winked at me and put her hands on my temples. "Close your eyes," she instructed. "Feel the magic." I obliged, and suddenly, I could feel a tingling, an unfamiliar sensation, but not unpleasant. "Do you feel it? Now, concentrate, and try and expand your sense of it." I felt her hands withdrawn, but I could still feel the magic in the air.

"I can still feel it," I told Rosaleth. "It's...it's softer, but I feel it."

"Good," she said. "Now, I want you to send out a call along it. Think of the magic a little bit like a spider's web—it's very delicate but if you're careful, you can send a tremor along it. Follow that tremor along, and you can sense the way the weave of magic in an area is."

I did as she suggested, and immediately noticed something that struck me as noteworthy.

"We're at some kind of crossing, aren't we? Like, the center of a web or something."

"We call it a nexus," Rosaleth said, pride in her voice. "You really do pick things up quickly."

"That's why we're doing this here, isn't it?" I guessed. "Because we can send a message out from here in all directions and it'll reach farther, instead of having to send it up one path and down another..."

"Partly," Rosaleth said. "There's more to it than that but for now we'll just leave it there. Now—I want you to focus on calling out for a familiar. Don't try to shape it—you want to leave the call as open as possible. If you try to call out for a certain animal but there's none suited to you, you'll get nowhere fast."

I focused as she instructed, and tried to send out the call. I felt a little self-conscious at first, uncertain if I was doing it right, but Rosaleth didn't step in to correct me, so I thought I must be doing all right. Then, after what seemed an interminably long time, I felt a tremor coming back.

"Good!" said Rosaleth. "You've done it! You can open your eyes now."

I did, and looked around for my familiar. Disappointingly, I saw no sign of them yet, though I did see that Constance was also looking around, while Silke was still focusing. Sara opened her eyes and began searching as well, and I winked at her.

A beat of wings heralded the arrival of the first new familiar, as a large raven flew from the woods and landed on Constance's shoulder. Constance looked insufferably smug to be the first whose familiar had arrived, and the smugness only grew as Mistress Eve spoke.

"A raven familiar is often a sign of a witch with a very strong fate, one who is destined for great things," she said. "Well done, Constance."

I could almost feel the smugness radiating from Constance at that point.

Silke opened her eyes, and—abruptly—a chipmunk scurried forward from the nearby underbrush. Silke let out a small squeal of delight as it obligingly climbed into her waiting hands.

"Chipmunk familiars are a sign of a witch who likes to be well prepared," Mistress Alina said. "Chipmunks seem flighty but they stockpile food for the winter, and thus don't go hungry. Good work,

Silke!" Silke beamed, already snuggling her familiar close.

I wondered for a moment why Silke's familiar had arrived before mine, when she had clearly been still calling out for it well after I had finished—Rosaleth leaned over and whispered in my ear the answer before I could voice the question.

"That chipmunk was already in the bushes," she whispered. "Your familiar seems to be coming from a little further away."

Sara's familiar arrived next, though, not mine—a cat, like Mistress Lirella's, but with white and black fur, rather than pure black.

"Cat familiars are the sign of a traditional witch," Mistress Lirella said with an air of pride—her apprentice, after all, was the only one so far with the same type of familiar as she herself had called. "I will say no more, to avoid the appearance of bragging—but well done, Sara."

Which left me to last. Despite what Rosaleth had assured me, I felt trepidation, as well as the eyes of my fellow apprentices upon me. I knew Constance, at least, would be judging me. Don't hold us back, she had said yesterday—somehow, I had the feeling that it was going to be a topic that would be revisited as soon as she could manage to do so without one of the adults around.

Then my familiar appeared. And she was beautiful—a fox, with bright red fur and black paws. *"I apologize for my tardiness,"* she said, *"but I thought it best to arrive fashionably late."*

"A fox familiar," Rosaleth said, grinning, "is a sign of an exceptionally clever witch, often a trickster or one who subverts fate. Well done, Tally, well done."

I hugged my new familiar, and grinned, forgetting all about Constance. I had done it!

Duties

For the most part the rest of that afternoon we spent with our familiars, getting to know them—which mostly involved hugs and cuddles, though less so for Constance, who seemed content to admire her raven without close physical contact.

"Did you hear that?" she said to no one in particular. "A raven familiar is a sign that I'll be a powerful witch."

I pretended I didn't hear her, focused as I was on naming my familiar.

"You don't have a name already, do you?" I asked hopefully, remembering Snickers' complaint about his name.

"I only gained the ability to think and speak in human terms when your call reached me," said the fox, her voice soothing and a little bit amused. *"I never really gave much thought to names until then. Please, just don't name me something silly or childish."*

I glanced around for inspiration. Sara had already declared her cat—black with small white splotches—to be named Starry. Constance seemed to be struggling with naming her raven as much as I was my fox. As for Silke, I didn't know either way whether she had settled on a name. I stood up and went over to ask her.

"Hey Silke," I asked, "have you got a name for your familiar yet?"

"Oh yes," she said, "this is Pipsie!"

"Pleased to make your acquaintance," Pipsie said. If the name bothered her, she didn't show it.

"That's a good name," I said, though I knew it wouldn't have suited my familiar.

"What about you?" Silke asked. "Have you got a name yet?"

I shook my head no. "Not yet," I said. "I'm having trouble thinking of a good one.

"Lord Ebonfeather," declared Constance, suddenly, from nearby. "That shall be your name!"

I noticed Silke rolling her eyes, and when she saw that I had noticed, she winked. I winked back.

"I'm fine without a name just now," my familiar said somewhat urgently. *"Especially if rushing into a name means being called Pipsie or Lady Redfur or something like that."*

"Hey now," I said, though privately I agreed that I would as soon not give her a cutesie name nor a melodramatic one. "Those are perfectly suitable names for someone else's familiar," I continued.

"But not yours," she said, somewhat smugly.

"But not mine," I agreed.

I still had not come up with a good name, though, when Mistress Eve called for our attention.

"You've taken a very important first step today, girls," she began. "But it's time we explain to you what being a witch fully entails. You will obviously learn about magic, and potions, and healing arts, but there is more than that to learn and there are responsibilities that come with the title of witch."

"The first, of course, is to be the wise woman for the town you'll be living in. This involves duties like helping to heal the sick and injured, but there are other, subtler ways in which a good witch will help her people. Careful matchmaking, for example, or settling arguments—never like a ruler, of course, but subtly, quietly. People will come to you for advice, and you must be willing and able to provide it—sometimes at all hours of the day. You'll experience this during your apprenticeship as well."

Now Mistress Lirella spoke. "The second duty of the witch is to intercede with supernatural forces that may come upon your village. Wandering magical creatures, the Fair Folk, and more can all be threats to the safety of those you watch over. But you must also remember that your duty includes watching over them as well— if a unicorn passes through your domain you should not just chase it off, but rather seek it out and determine if it needs your assistance. The Fair Folk especially can be dangerous but will always adhere to their agreements, so if a band of them begins marauding you can be sure that somewhere an agreement has been broken—you may be able to bring a peaceful end to the conflict by finding out the terms of the agreement that have not been upheld and remedying the situation, or by negotiating a new agreement."

Mistress Alina spoke next. "The third duty of the witch is to help other witches when they call upon you. You are not alone in the world, and no one witch has the power to act as the witches of old did, reshaping entire kingdoms to their whims, turning people to newts, or the like, not anymore. When a fellow witch comes to you for aid, you must always be willing to assist, lest when you need assistance none will come to answer your call."

Rosaleth was the last to speak. "The fourth, and final duty of the witch is to preserve magic in the world, and where possible, bring forth new magics. Your time not spent on your other duties will be spent on researching enchantments, tracking down lost magics, and sharing your knowledge with other witches."

"Are there any questions?" Mistress Eve asked.

"The Fair Folk—they're real?" Silke asked, raising her hand hesitantly.

"They are," Mistress Eve said. "Most of the time they're not too dangerous, as long as you remember never to say anything that could be interpreted as a promise unless you really mean to keep it. They'll hold you to it, but they follow the same rules. If you can get them to agree to something, they'll hold to the letter of the agreement until the other side is broken."

That seemed in keeping with the stories I'd always heard of fairies. I resolved to be very very cautious of saying anything, should I ever encounter one of the Fair Folk.

"You mentioned lost magics, Mistress Rosaleth," Sara said. "Is so much lost to us?"

Rosaleth nodded with a sigh. "Once, as you know, witches had the power to do more, far more. Some witches abused that power to become powerful enchantresses or witch-queens in their own right, choosing to rule rather than advise, or trying to shape the fate of entire kingdoms into what they believed were better outcomes. The trouble is that even if you think you know best for a kingdom, if you ever lose sight of that, or lose control of the weave of magic, disaster can strike. Look at the tale of the Briar Rose—a conflict between witches led to an entire kingdom being sealed in unnatural sleep and a wall of thorns until the spell could be broken. The details of the story are inaccurate at best, now, but it is exactly the sort of thing that used to happen. There may still be other kingdoms in stasis out there, lost until the right conditions are met to bring them back."

"There are also," Mistress Lirella said, "quite a large variety of magic items out in the world. Cauldrons that produce gruel on command, as long as you keep stirring the pot, magic swords that make the holder unbeatable in combat, even flying carpets. Most of them are unassuming but dangerous without the proper commands, if activated unwittingly. A few years ago a magical sword was found in a chest in the attic of a farmer—his great grandfather had wielded it in battle, until he was laid low by a scratch of a nettle that became badly infected. It's part of our job to find such items and keep them safe."

"It sounds like we'll be very busy." Constance sniffed. "And it sounds like a lot of these duties will be thankless jobs."

"If you only wished to become a witch for the accolades you would earn," Mistress Eve said to Constance coldly, "then I sorely misjudged you. I'm disappointed, Constance."

Constance flushed red with embarrassment. "That isn't what I meant—" she protested, but Mistress Eve held up a hand.

"We've clearly given you all a lot to think about already. It's no good to overwhelm you with too much to take in, so that will end today's lesson. Constance, come with me, please."

Constance, looking pale now, followed Mistress Eve away from the wagon. Mistress Alina and Silke went to move the wagon off the road and unhitch the horses—it seemed we would be "camping" here tonight.

Rosaleth disappeared into the wagon once it had been moved, and didn't come back out for some time. I assumed if she'd wanted my accompaniment she would have asked, so I sat down and leaned back against a rock. On an impulse, I closed my eyes and tried to sense the magic again.

It was difficult at first, but after a few moments I could feel the weave—the nexus we were in like a crossroads on a map, or like the center of a spider's web. I sent a probing tremor along the nearest thread, and to my surprise I could "see" other tangles of magic moving around. One of them climbed into my lap—my familiar, I could immediately tell, as something about her felt immediately comfortable and, yes, familiar, to my fledgling magical senses. Nearby I could sense a very large bundle of tightly wrapped threads, which I took to be the wagon. I saw a pair of...well, I could tell they were alive, and I guessed they were Silke and Mistress Alina based on their position and the way they were moving around. Off a little ways I could also sense what I assumed to be Sara and Mistress Lirella, both quite still. Beyond them, I strained to see if I could detect Constance and Mistress Eve, but my concentration broke as Sara's voice sounded in my mind.

"*Tally!*" she said. My eyes snapped open, and I saw her across the campsite, where I'd sensed her sitting before. She was grinning at me, her dark eyes twinkling. "*It worked! I thought I'd see if we could talk like our familiars do, through the weave.*"

I was more than a little surprised. "How..." I wondered aloud.

"*It's not as hard as it looks,*" my familiar assured me. "*You were doing it just fine when you called for me, after all.*"

I thought for a few moments about this, and closed my eyes. "*Sara?*" I sent hesitantly. She gave a little wave.

"*I knew you'd figure it out quickly too,*" she said in my mind. "*I wonder if the others can hear us too...?*"

I looked at Mistress Lirella, who showed no sign of awareness of the conversation. If she could hear us, she was doing a good job of hiding it. Which, given that it was Mistress Lirella, wouldn't have surprised me, admittedly, but I saw no reason that she would not praise Sara's ingenuity if she was able to hear us.

"*Well I bet we could tell Silke and Constance how to do this,*" I said, "*so that we can talk to each other even if we're busy doing other things, or—well, there's a lot of ways we could use this, anyway.*" With the duties we'd just been told about, I could think of many ways that talking silently to someone else would come in handy. "*We should probably mention that we figured this out to our mistresses, too,*" I added almost regretfully. One of the duties was, after all, to share lost magics, and if our mistresses didn't know this could be done then we had an obligation to tell them.

"*They'd just tell us we can't do it,*" Sara said. "*It's bad enough you want to give it to Constance.*"

"*Think of how insufferable she'd be if she found out later we've been able to do this the entire time,*" I said, "*and, think how much it'll bother her that you and I figured this out before she did.*"

Sara grinned wickedly. "*All right, you make a good point. I'll share it with Silke and Constance, then. But we don't tell our mistresses, not yet. We'll tell them later, once we've learned more about it.*"

I couldn't say I liked keeping secrets, especially from Rosaleth, but my familiar rested her head on my hands and seemed to approve of the plan.

"*By the way, did you come up with a name for your familiar yet?*"

Sara asked.

I glanced at my fox, and smiled.

"Secret," I said.

Doubts

Rosaleth eventually emerged from the wagon when Mistress Alina and Silke started making preparations for dinner and needed into the larder, chasing her out of the wagon in the process. Rosaleth grumbled about it but didn't look too displeased. She looked around, saw me, and came over, crouching beside where I sat against a tree.

"Remember that potion I told you about?" she asked, "The one that you'll have to drink every day? One spoonful of this, at dinner." She pressed a bottle into my hands. "Every day."

I threw my arms around Rosaleth in a hug, then realized that might be a little bit too far and withdrew. She looked rather embarrassed by it.

"Hey now," she said.

"Sorry," I said, scratching my head. "I was just...thank you."

"Don't thank me too much. You haven't smelled it yet. We're going to have to air out the wagon after dinner."

Constance and Mistress Eve returned in time for dinner to be served. Our cheerful cooks, Mistress Alina and Silke, presented us with a hearty stew, thick-brothed and full of beef and potatoes. As I tucked in, I had a thought.

"What do our familiars eat?" I asked. "Can they eat...people food?"

"*I certainly would enjoy a portion of whatever it is that you're eating,*" Secret said. "*It smells absolutely magnificent.*"

Silke and Mistress Alina laughed, and Mistress Alina rose to dish out a bowlful of stew—heavy on the meat—for my familiar.

"It usually depends on the familiar," Mistress Alina said, "and what they ate before. Miss Geraldine usually just eats flies, for example.

"*A perfectly healthy diet,*" said her familiar in a slightly indignant tone.

"I never said otherwise," soothed Mistress Alina. "It was simply an example."

"Well done for considering the care of your familiar, Tally," Mistress Eve said. I was surprised by the compliment, or rather, its source—it had been my impression that Mistress Eve didn't much like me. Perhaps that had been through association with Constance, though.

Constance herself had been rather subdued since returning to our camp site with Mistress Eve. I assumed that Mistress Eve had said something to her in the intervening time, since she made none of her usual effort to one-up the rest of us—myself in particular— or any of her other usual, less-than-charming behavior. I was still intimidated by Constance's mistress, but I had to admit my impression of her was improving.

"They would have started complaining eventually," said Mistress Alina with a chuckle, setting out a few more dishes of food for the other familiars. We all thanked her for having planned ahead—as she evidently had known the topic would come up.

After dinner, I uncorked the potion Rosaleth had spent the afternoon brewing for me. She was right, I decided, wrinkling my nose, it did smell terrible. Still, it would help me become who I wanted to be, so I dutifully tipped out a spoonful and, holding my nose, gulped it down.

"What's that, Tally?" Silke asked.

"Medicine," I said, not really sure if I should elaborate.

"I didn't know you were sick," Silke said. She cocked her head to one side. "I'm sorry."

"It's not that I'm sick," I said, trying to think how best to approach the subject. "I was...It's more that I need some help getting my body to be the way it should be."

"Oh." Silke clearly didn't really want to press further, sensing my reluctance. "Well, if you need something to wash it down, I can make some sweet drink for you," she said. "I bet it tastes as bad as it smells!"

"Worse," I said with a nod. "Maybe something sweet would help. Thanks, Silke."

Silke smiled back at me. "We're friends, right? There's nothing better than helping a friend."

After dinner, as predicted, the wagon did need to be aired out for awhile. The witches seemed to reach an agreement to use this time for a bit of further teaching. Rosaleth beckoned me over to the tree I had been sitting against before, and we sat together beneath it.

"So," she said, "first day doing real magic. How do you feel?"

"It's...overwhelming, a little bit. Even though we didn't do much, I mean, I have a familiar now."

"Well excuse me for not being much to do," Secret said. Her tail twitched as she melodramatically turned her back to me. The effect was somewhat ruined when she glanced over her shoulder back at me a moment later to see my reaction.

"See what I mean about the sarcasm?" Rosaleth asked as Snickers made a rude noise in our heads. "So, overwhelmed. Not actually a bad reaction, given the dangers inherent in playing with forces you don't fully understand. What'd you do while I was brewing your potion?" She seemed casual, but at the same time there was an intensity there that made me glad I had an answer.

"I tried to focus on what you showed me before," I said, "the threads of magic. The...weave?" I wasn't sure if that was the right word.

"Ley lines," Rosaleth said. "They're called ley lines. They criss-cross the land, sparse in some places, dense in others. Where they cross is called a locus, and where there are many loci in one spot, we call it a nexus."

I nodded to show my understanding of the new words. "So this is a nexus?" I asked.

"A small one," Rosaleth said. "Big enough to work a bit of bigger magic, and a good spot for something like calling a familiar. The really big ones are called Grand Nexus, and they're very important places. Most of them are either lost, ruined, or occupied."

"How would they be ruined?" I asked.

"Ley lines are shaped by the land," she said. "That includes things like buildings. In the old days there were a lot less big cities and such compared to now, but when people found a Grand Nexus it usually became a center for activity, and eventually if a city grew up around it it would be disrupted."

"But wouldn't we have wanted to stop that from happening, if we knew it could?"

"Part of our job is to help people," she said. "It's hard to do that if we have to keep telling them they can't live where they want—hard enough keeping them away from places that are actually dangerous. Also, the fewer places with a Grand Nexus, the fewer chances there are for some maniac to decide she should be queen and enforce that with magic." She shrugged. "It seemed like a worthwhile tradeoff, I guess."

I nodded again. For a few moments, Rosaleth was quiet, letting me digest what she had told me.

I swallowed, then asked, "May I ask a question?"

"You just did, but go ahead." Rosaleth grinned at me.

"Why did you choose me to be your apprentice?" I asked.

"What's brought this on?" Rosaleth asked. She looked surprised at the question.

"Well, I just wondered, because I know you hadn't been planning to take an apprentice—I heard Mistress Eve say so, and everyone knew there were only three apprentices being chosen anyway. And I just, I didn't know why me, when you would rather have had no apprentice at all."

"Hey," Rosaleth said, poking me gently in the shoulder. "You're my apprentice because I wanted you to be my apprentice, and that's way better than no apprentice at all." She leaned back against the tree, looking up.

"Truth is, I'm not the best teacher," she said. "I should have given you something to do before I went off to brew the potion for you, but I plumb forgot. You did something anyway with it, and probably figured out a lot more by yourself than I would have had you work on. You're a clever girl, and that makes the difference."

"But you still didn't have to take me on as an apprentice just because I'm clever, or because you saw that I was a girl when no one else knew," I said, still thinking about Constance's claim that I was probably a charity case. "For all you knew I was just a clever thief."

"I liked that, too. You're braver than you know, Tally, and clever, and not afraid to break rules sometimes. You'll make a great witch." Rosaleth smiled encouragingly at me. "Just ask Secret."

"Of course I agree," Secret said. *"Who'd want to be a familiar to an inferior witch, after all?"*

Suddenly I felt tears on my face. Crying again, like a little child. Rosaleth hugged me comfortingly.

"Don't you worry, Tally. You're not just some stray I picked up—you're my apprentice. Even if I didn't think I'd want one, you proved me wrong."

I bawled for a little while before calming down. I realized that Constance and the other girls had seen me crying, too, and worried for a moment before deciding that I really didn't care. Let Constance try to say something if she liked—I knew that she wasn't the only clever one, and I had Rosaleth and Silke and Sara to rely on as well. She saw me looking at her and looked away, nonchalantly.

She'd been wrong, and I knew it. I wasn't a charity case after all.

Fortunes

The next day we started out early, after a delicious breakfast of pancakes. Mistress Alina and Silke had mixed blueberries into them to add a bit of extra flavor. I started washing the dishes without having to be asked, and Sara joined in to help me dry them, as we had done yesterday. Constance was still subdued and quiet, for which I was silently grateful as well.

As the wagon rolled along, we were treated to an impromptu lesson in herbalism by Mistress Lirella, who was taking stock of the supply on the wagon—and finding it depleted in apparently unexpected ways.

I kept to myself that I knew where some of the herbs had gone. If Rosaleth had wanted Mistress Lirella to know, she would have mentioned, after all.

"We'll have to stop," Mistress Lirella said. "There's a good herbalist in the town of Sevenbridge a few miles up the road, as I recall, and we can resupply there."

"Oh come on, Lirella," Rosaleth said, "we don't actually need most of those herbs right now anyway. We can explain to the girls what they do without needing to have them on hand."

Mistress Lirella shook her head in disagreement. "When we took possession of the Wagon, it was fully stocked, and I intend to see it returned the same way. Additionally, I'm not entirely inclined to trust that the herb garden in the cottage I'm to reside in has been properly cared for, and want to be sure that I have certain specific plants on hand. It's as good an opportunity as any to ensure that we have what we're going to need in our new homes."

"That's a good point." Rosaleth nodded her agreement. "The girls probably wouldn't mind a chance to get out of the wagon and see Sevenbridge, either, I'm betting."

We all sat up a little straighter at that thought. It had been a long time since I'd been to a new place, and Sevenbridge was a real town, not just a village like Tancred's Ford. It must be somewhat noteworthy if Mistress Lirella knew of an herbalist that lived here specifically.

"Please, can we?" Constance said, breaking her silence. "I'd love to go shopping in Sevenbridge."

"Well, you'll have to talk to Eve," Rosaleth said, "but I think it should be okay, provided you girls stay together and don't wander off alone." Mistress Eve was currently taking her turn driving the Wagon.

"Well this should be fun," Sara's voice sounded in my mind, dripping sarcasm. *"We'll get to follow Constance around all afternoon. Yay."*

"Be nice," I sent back to her. *"She's been better since yesterday."*

"I guess," Sara said. She sounded unconvinced, and I couldn't really blame her—even though it was me, more than her, who seemed to bear the brunt of Constance's dislike, Constance was more than capable of being insufferable to everyone. We'd just have to put up with it if we wanted to go out on the town, though.

As it happened, when we finally reached Sevenbridge an hour or two before dinner, the witches all agreed that we should be allowed to spend a little time in the town market, and gave us each a small allowance, with the admonition to return in time for dinner, and to stay together at all times. Silke was hesitant, wanting to help Mistress Alina with cooking, but Mistress Alina just laughed her infectious laugh and told her to go and have fun with her friends.

We accompanied Mistress Lirella and Rosaleth to the market square, where they had business with the herbalist. Mistress Eve and Mistress Alina had provided shopping lists of their own, but Mistress Eve had declined to come into town herself, citing tiredness, and Mistress Alina was busy with dinner, leaving the other two witches to collect their shopping for them.

"I just hope this herbalist is as good as you say," Rosaleth said as we came to the shop. "All right, girls, meet us back here in an hour or so."

We chorused our agreement and watched Rosaleth and Mistress Lirella go inside the herbalist's shop. I rather wanted to go inside as well and see what a well stocked herbalist might have, but the others seemed disinterested in that after spending all day learning about herbs in the Wagon, so I simply sighed and followed them around as we wandered the square. There were a lot more people here than I'd ever seen in one place before, most of them busily hurrying from one place to another with no time to stop to chat. It seemed less friendly than Tancred's Ford, despite the variety of shops and stalls that lined the market square.

"I saw a bakery earlier," said Silke. "We could go and get some sweets."

"We'd just ruin our appetites for dinner," Sara said. "I'd rather go look at that bookstore over there."

"I've had enough of learning for one day." Silke groaned. "What else is there?"

"We could try that?" Constance's voice was quiet, but she pointed at a sign on small shop window, nestled between a butcher's shop and a shoemaker, that read, *Fortunes Told.*

"Good idea," I said. "That sounds like more fun than bookstores or sweets—it's something we never had back home. Right?"

Constance gave me a look, but seeing I was sincere, only nodded. The others thought it over for a few moments and then nodded too.

"Well spotted, Constance," Sara said.

Silke giggled. "I wonder if any of our fortunes will involve cute boys," she said in a dreamy tone. "I hope mine does!"

We entered the shop and found it to be set up as a small sitting room, with a little old lady just finishing making a pot of tea within. The smell of mint was strong, and there was a bowl of mint candies on a side table.

"Welcome, girls," she said. Her voice was kindly, as was her appearance and manner. "You've come to have your fortunes read? Sit, please, have a nice cup of tea, and let me get my cards." She poured each of us a cup of tea, then sat down opposite us at the table and produced a deck of cards from somewhere I didn't quite spot. "Which of you will be first?" she asked.

"Oh, me!" Silke said. Constance looked slightly nonplussed, having clearly wanted to be first, and I coughed gently.

"It was Constance's idea to come in, Silke," I said. "She should be allowed to be first."

I wasn't sure why I was being nice to Constance. She'd never been nice to me—but I didn't want to be cruel to her in return just because of that. Constance gave me a calculating glance, but didn't object as I thought she might. Instead, she silently slid the coins she had been given by Mistress Eve across the table to the old lady.

"Okaaaaaaay." Silke's pout was a little too cutesy to be anything but affected, and she watched with interest as the fortune telling began.

The kindly old lady held the cards out to Constance. "Please shuffle the cards, focusing on your question" she said. Constance obligingly shuffled and handed them back.

I leaned forward to get a better look as the kindly old lady laid out three cards face-down, then set the rest of the deck aside.

"This card represents your past," she said, turning over the first card. I saw it was a picture of a blonde girl gazing out a window, with a legend reading *The Dreamer*. "You have longed for something your whole life," said the old lady, "but you have not felt able to reach that goal."

She turned over the next card, this one showing a young boy assisting an older man at a forge. It was labelled *The Apprentice*. "This card is your present. You're finally able to learn and move towards your goal, but it may be a long time coming, or hard work, to achieve it. You must keep sight of your goal—do not despair, for the Apprentice can signify a reward at the end of a long road."

She turned over the final card, showing a witch in a beautiful black dress, with animals surrounding her. I had to look closer to notice that the animals all seemed to be bowing. The card was labelled *The Sorceress*. The fortune-teller spoke again. "The Sorceress—you will achieve the goal you seek, but you must be careful. The Sorceress represents power, but also pride. Remember that as you near your goal."

Constance nodded eagerly. Silke and Sara looked impressed, and I couldn't deny that I felt a little bit of surprise at how the fortune Constance had received was clearly in response to the question I was sure she'd focused on while shuffling the cards.

"Now, dearies, which one of you would like to go next?"

Silke's enthusiasm was clear, so I sat back to allow her the next reading. I was pretty sure she was going to ask about romance, and her reading was, like Constance's, eerily on point. *The Dreamer* appeared again as the card of the past, with *The Hart* as the present—a pursuit, the old fortune-teller said, or one pursued. It showed a white stag with magnificent antlers, but also a hunter behind a tree nearby. The final card, that of the future, was *The Commitment*, which showed a couple swearing wedding vows, but, the old lady warned, could also represent commitments other than marriage, despite the illustration of the card, such as commitment to a duty or to an ideal. Silke didn't seem to be bothered by that—she was clearly as satisfied with her fortune as Constance had been.

The fortune-teller turned to Sara and I then. "Well, dearies?" She offered the cards to us.

"Thank you, but I think I will pass today," Sara said. "I just came to be with my friends."

I hesitated. I wasn't really sure what question I wanted answered, but I knew I was fascinated. After a moment, I slid my allowance across the table and accepted the deck, closing my eyes and trying to focus on a question as I shuffled. I still couldn't think of a great question to ask beyond a vague interest in the future, but a sudden instinct flared and I concentrated on sensing the leylines—and nearly dropped the cards in surprise. The shop was a nexus! What was more, I could feel the cards drawing from the leylines as I shuffled them—not exactly magic the way the Wagon was, but this confirmed that there was something more to them than just a fanciful prop. I opened my eyes, finished shuffling, and passed the cards back to the fortune teller.

I swear, she winked at me as she laid out the three cards. The first one she turned over nearly made me gasp. It depicted a fox, looking almost identical to Secret, and was labelled *The Trickster*.

"Your past," the fortune teller said. "The Trickster. One who is not bound by the restrictions of expectation—one who subverts fate." I could feel the other girls shiver along with me at that phrase, the same that Rosaleth had used to describe a witch with a fox familiar. I sat up a little straighter.

"Your present," said the fortune teller, turning the next card over. Like Constance, I had drawn The Apprentice. "You are learning, growing, and moving towards your goal. It may be a hard road, but perseverance will be rewarded."

I couldn't help leaning forward as she turned the final card. To my surprise, it was blank white, with no illustration or label at all.

"The future unwritten," the fortune teller said, with surprise evident on her face. "The fate unspoken. I thought I had...no, it matters not. May I ask your name, young lady?"

"Tally," I said, not sure how to react to this.

"Tally," said the old fortune teller, "your future is your own to make. I am just an old woman with a gift for fortune cards, but you—all of you—will be something greater." She scooped up the cards and passed them back over to me. "I give you these fortune cards, Tally. In all my years, I have never seen a reading such as yours, and I suspect you will have use for them."

I looked at my friends, surprised. Their faces mirrored my own shock.

"Thank you," I said.

"Are the cards magical?" Silke asked.

"No, and yes," the old woman said, rising and moving to put a CLOSED sign in her window. "They are not themselves magical, but I suspect Tally will be able to make good use of the cards." She smiled at me again. "Remember what you saw, young Tally, and you will make an excellent fortune teller yourself someday if you choose, though I suspect that will be the least of what you accomplish. Now, please excuse me, dearies, I find myself drained and must rest."

We filed out of the shop. Constance gave me a stare. "I see you're the special one yet again," she said. Her voice was more bitter than angry.

"Hey, she did say you'd become a powerful witch—that's good too, right?" My protest was weak even to my own ears—after all, it was me who had been given the deck of fortune cards, not Constance.

Constance sighed. "Just don't think that I'm going to give up just because you're special," she said. "I'll prove that I'm the better witch. You'll see."

"I don't want to be better than anyone," I said, but Constance was already moving away, back to the herbalist shop, where I could see that Rosaleth and Mistress Lirella were waiting for us, laden with jars of herbs and a few live plants.

"I don't," I said again to no one in particular. Sara squeezed my shoulder and Silke smiled.

"Don't worry," Sara said. "She'll get over it."

I wasn't sure she would, but I didn't argue.

Cards

"What did you girls do while we were busy haggling for all of this stuff?" Rosaleth asked conversationally as we hiked back to the Wagon. Evidently she had come out on the poor end of the deal, at least in her own opinion. Mistress Lirella was largely ignoring Rosaleth's complaints with an air of long-suffering patience, which meant that Mistress Lirella was effectively ignoring Rosaleth entirely. In desperation for conversation, Rosaleth was apparently turning to us instead.

"We got our fortunes told!" said Silke. "Constance is going to be a powerful witch," she said, lowering her voice conspiratorially as she related the details, as though gossiping. Which, in a way, she was. "I'm going to meet a cute boy and fall in love, and Tally, you won't believe what hers was! The fortune teller even gave her the fortune cards!"

Rosaleth was smiling and laughing at the first two fortunes Silke revealed, but she raised her eyebrow when she heard about my fortune, and looked more than a little surprised to hear that I had been given a fortune deck. I had thought she might be angry for us for meddling in something that actually did seem to have power, or worse, force me to give up the cards—which I was already fond of, thanks to the Trickster card's illustration. I was unprepared for her to be interested and pleased by the development.

"May I see the cards, Tally? What was your fortune?"

"Well, sure," I said, handing her the deck. "I got the Trickster card, the one that looks like Secret, and then the Apprentice, and then the blank card."

Mistress Lirella made a little exclamation of surprise. "An extraordinary reading," she said. "It suggests—well, it suggests that Mistress Rosaleth was right to choose you to become one of us, Tally. Sara, what was your fortune?" she asked.

"I didn't have it told," Sara said. "I thought it was all a bit silly before Tally's, actually—it was a lot like she was telling Constance and Sara just what they wanted to hear, so I decided it was some kindly-looking old lady with a gift for reading people." A perfectly sensible answer—and in retrospect, before I had realized that the shop was a nexus, I would have thought so as well.

Mistress Lirella, however, looked disappointed. "Even if it was a grift, that's half the fun of having your fortune told," she said. "We'll have to teach Tally to use those cards, now, so she can perform a reading for you."

"This is a nice deck," Rosaleth said, passing it back to me. "You might be right, Lirella. She's really into this stuff," she said in a stage whisper to us girls.

"I certainly am," Mistress Lirella said. "I never understood why it isn't taught more often, as it is often surprisingly accurate, even when the reading is performed by someone with no mastery of magic. It should be studied and shared." Her enthusiasm was a new side to her that I had not seen before—almost girlish. It made her seem more approachable, somehow.

"It's hedge magic, parlor tricks," Rosaleth said. "It's unreliable—though if Tally is right and there was a nexus, there may well be something to the readings the girls were given. The big reason is that it's too much like controlling fates, and you know what comes from trying to do that." She didn't sound like she was particularly against the idea, but was clearly less impressed by it than Mistress Lirella.

"What is hedge magic?" Constance asked quietly. "Is it bad?"

"Not everyone who uses magic is a witch, obviously," Mistress Lirella said, her tone returning to her usual calm. "There are wizards, of course, and certain groups of monster hunters, who use magic similar to what we do. But there are some kinds of magic that can be used by common folk with no gift otherwise. We call these, 'hedge magics.'" She paused.

"Hedge magics aren't good or bad," Rosaleth said, picking up the explanation. "They're just there. Most of the time, we witches can do the same thing more effectively another way, or for various reasons don't want much to do with them. They're not things we want to be doing—like, making love potions? Forbidden. Outright. But fortune cards, they're just...not always clear or useful until in hindsight, when it's too late—and often as not that hindsight is twisting the way a reading went to make it fit the facts."

"They're more accurate if used correctly, of course." Mistress Lirella sniffed. "Tally, you said you noticed the shop was a nexus—did you notice anything about the cards at the same time?"

"Well," I said, "they were sort of drawing from the way I was focusing on the future. I think that, because I was focusing on that, they were able to somehow..." I gestured vaguely, unable to formulate into words the thought that I was trying to express. The cards had been doing something, that was sure, but it hadn't felt like magic, just...something.

"You felt it, then," Mistress Lirella said. "That happens sometimes, even when neither the reader nor the subject is aware of ley lines and lack the ability to perform magic entirely."

"That 'sometimes' is the reason it's hedge magic." Rosaleth said. Mistress Lirella gave her a dirty look.

"I was coming to that," she said. "But yes, that's right. So it's not usually taught to witches. If Tally would like to learn, I would be happy to teach her."

"I might as well," I said, noticing that even Sara seemed excited now. "I mean, I have these cards, I may as well learn to use them, right? I'm still surprised she just gave them to me."

"I hope you thanked her," Rosaleth said. "It's a tradition, actually—you're not supposed to buy or sell fortune cards. Traditionally, they are always given as a gift or created for oneself."

"Won't that mean that the fortune teller has to retire now?" Silke asked, worry evident on her face.

"Probably not," Rosaleth said. "If she doesn't have a spare set, I'd be surprised—besides, she probably made those herself. I haven't seen a deck like that before."

"Very likely," Mistress Lirella said. "They are quite nice. Tally is lucky indeed." She sounded a bit jealous of the deck, but only a bit.

Constance, on the other hand...Constance was not looking happy with me at all. I sighed. It wasn't like I was asking for any of this! I had no idea what I could do to ease the tension between us, but if I didn't do something eventually I would have to deal with Constance's rivalry growing worse and worse.

Mistress Alina gave us a big smile when we returned to the camp. "You're just in time,' she said. "I was starting to worry that I would need to serve dinner cold!" She dished out our portions—a bit of pork with gravy, mashed potatoes and peas—and we all tucked in.

We filled Mistress Alina and Mistress Eve in as we ate. Mistress Alina was excited and entertained by the recounting of our fortunes, and Mistress Eve looked thoughtfully at Constance—and at me.

"I want to see this card," Secret said, interrupting my train of thought. *"The one that apparently looks like me."* I showed it to her, and she regarded it for a few moments, then said, *"Mm, yes. I can see the resemblance—but I smell better."*

"Are you going to show us how to do a reading?" Silke asked Mistress Lirella eagerly once we had finished cleaning up after dinner, and were all sitting around the woodstove in the Wagon. "Show Tally, I mean."

I hid a smile. Silke obviously wanted to have her future read again, and ask more questions about boys.

"Oh, she can't just use Tally's cards," said Mistress Alina—evidently she was also keen on fortune cards. "That's a big no-no with fortune cards. Only the owner can get an accurate reading with them. Tally would have to give them as a gift to Lirella, and I'm sure the little dear doesn't want to do that, do you?"

I shook my head. "I can try, though," I said. "Um, it was just three cards, right? Past, present, and future?"

"That's one spread," said Mistress Eve. "A relatively simple one—not quite the simplest. The more complicated you get when you choose your spread, the more you can tell about a person or situation, but the more room there is for misinterpretation. There's dozens of ways to lay the cards out, and dozens of ways to interpret every card." She shrugged. "It's part of why I don't set much stock in them."

"Oh pooh," said Mistress Alina. "You're no fun, just like Rosaleth. Tally, if you really want the simplest of readings, you can just draw focus on a question and draw one card. The card is supposed to tell you something useful about the question."

"But I don't know what most of the cards mean," I said. "How can I tell from just the picture?"

"The illustration is meant to be evocative of the card's symbolism and interpretations," Mistress Lirella said. "The amateur reader is meant to be able to discern those meanings for themselves through this."

"So I just, think of a question, and draw a card, and it's that simple?" I asked.

"The most basic reading is. Then there's the three-card spread, which you saw, several cruciform readings, and others. Some readers invent their own unique spreads," Mistress Lirella said.

"Make it up as they go, you mean," Mistress Rosaleth said. "Tally, the important part is to focus, both while you're asking the question, and when you're interpreting the answer."

"I still feel like I'm not ready," I said. "At least...not in front of everyone." I was sure Constance would find some way to make any little mistake I might make into a point in her favor, somehow. She may have been quiet since yesterday, but she was still out to prove herself better than me.

Silke looked a little disappointed. "So no more fortune readings tonight?" she asked.

"Sorry," I said. "Once I've had a little more practice, I promise." This seemed to mollify her, and she smiled beatifically at me.

"I'll hold you to that!" she said.

Fair Folk

I sat in the back of the Wagon the next day as we travelled on, working on writing a letter to Shalla and Uncle Grim. We were all huddled inside, save for Rosaleth—it was pouring rain outside, but it was her turn to drive the Wagon and no amount of pleading or offering favors had been able to convince the other witches to take her place. I had offered to keep her company, but she had merely sighed and told me that there was no reason the both of us should be miserable, and so I had stayed inside.

It had only been a few days since I'd become Rosaleth's apprentice and already so many amazing things had happened to me! I had to be careful, though—we were coming up into a rockier part of the hills, and the road was getting a little bumpy, and I could only imagine that it was made worse by the weather. I'd already ruined one letter when ink spilled all over it.

"What are you writing, Tally?" Constance asked, peering at me from where she sat on the other side of the wagon.

"I'm writing to my sister and my uncle," I said. I was surprised she took an interest, but if she was going to be polite, so was I.

"Do you miss them?" she asked.

I nodded. "Very much," I said.

"I miss my parents too, a little" she said. "But I'm more worried that they'll be sad without me around. They're terribly fond of me, after all."

I remembered the night of the feast, and seeing Constance's mother crying to see her go—and I remembered that Constance herself had looked like she was holding back tears.

"Since I'm writing anyway," I said, "you could write something short to let them know you're okay, and I could put it in with my letter for Uncle Grim to give your family for you." I said it nonchalantly, as though it were an off-handed idea.

Constance stared at me for a few moments, eyes narrowing as she tried to guess my angle. Finally, she seemed to decide I wasn't trying to play any games, and her expression relaxed.

"I might do that, then," she said, as nonchalant as I had been a few moments before. "Thanks, Tally."

"Oh, can I do that too?" Silke asked me. "Send a letter with yours, I mean. I want Mama and Papa to know I'm okay."

"Sure," I said. "How about you, Sara?"

Sara shook her head, holding up a long letter she was already working on. "I've got too much to slip in with your letter, I think," she said. "But thank you."

I noticed Mistress Eve looking at me, her expression unreadable. When she saw that I had noticed, she gave a small nod.

"We've stopped," said Mistress Alina. I realized she was right— the Wagon had stopped moving.

Rosaleth clambered in from outside, drenched and looking none too pleased. "The bridge is out," she said. "It looks like a rotting timber gave way. We'll have to go another route."

The other witches all groaned at once.

"That means a day back to the Sevenbridge crossroads and another day across the lowland route, and then the long way back into the hills," Mistress Eve said. "Three days, at least. We weren't supposed to have the Wagon for anywhere near that long."

"The Grand Coven will understand," Mistress Alina said. "It's outside our control. It's far too soon to try and teach the girls flying, and heading back through Sevenbridge will at least give us a chance to let them know the bridge is out."

I glanced at my fellow apprentices in shock and surprise at the mention of flying—they all looked as excited and surprised as I felt. Were the stories of witches flying on brooms more than just tall tales after all? I'd assumed they were, since we were travelling in the Wagon, but now it seemed like I may have been wrong.

"Oh they know it's out," Rosaleth said. "There's a sign posted. I barely spotted it in the rain. You're forgetting there's another route we could take, though."

"Through the fey woods?" Mistress Lirella asked. "It's danger-ous, but it would keep us on schedule to return the Wagon. I don't care for the idea of bringing our apprentices into contact with the Fair Folk so early, but the Wagon may not actually have enough magic to carry us through the longer route."

"I'd forgotten about that," said Mistress Alina, concerned. "Do we at least know the right agreements and treaties to cite when we go through?"

Mistress Lirella frowned. "They should be in one of the books in the Wagon's library," she said. "Obviously we'll need to refer to them before we decide what to do."

Rosaleth shrugged, still dripping. "Whatever we're going to do," she said, "I'd just as soon wait till this storm dies down a little bit before trying to turn the wagon around."

The others absently agreed, clearly focusing more on preparing for travelling through the fey woods for the moment.

"Tell the girls what they'll need to know, then," Mistress Eve said to Rosaleth. "And get dry. You look like a drowned ferret."

Rosaleth made a rude noise—surprisingly close to the one that Snickers made at her when she teased him—and fetched herself a towel, then came to sit by the wood stove, beckoning us closer.

"We're going to be going through the fey woods," she said. "I'm sure you heard that. It's dangerous, but not so dangerous that you need to worry too much, if we're careful."

"What are the fairies like?" Silke asked. I could see she was excited, but the talk of danger was placing a damper on her usual enthusiasm.

Rosaleth grimaced. "First lesson: never call them fairies. They're the Fair Folk when you're referring to them as a whole, or if you know their individual types, ranks, and names, those are acceptable as well. For now, just stick to the Fair Folk. They're...prickly, but they're always fair. For a certain value of fair, anyway. They'll always hold to the letter of any agreement they make, but they're easily offended and very powerful, so we don't want to make them angry."

We spent the next little while learning about the etiquette that would be expected of us. While we were travelling through the fey woods, we would be riding outside the wagon—it would be awkward, Rosaleth admitted, but we did not want to give the impression that we were trying to hide anyone from them.

"We'll be watched the entire time," Rosaleth said, "but chances are we'll only be confronted the once. The highest ranking Fair Folk in the area will be the ones who come to meet us. You'll speak only when spoken to, and answer questions directly with as little embellishment as possible. Don't ask them any questions—they like to make bargains over answers and I don't want any of you getting into any bargains with the Fair Folk until you understand fully what you're doing. Let us do the talking as much as you can."

"What if they ask us something that we don't know the answer to?" Sara asked.

"Don't lie or try to guess," Rosaleth said. "Other than that, we'll try to keep things as short as possible. We're just passing through their territory, nothing else, and witches and the Fair Folk have old agreements to cover things like this."

"If we have agreements with them, why would they try to trick us or catch us up?" I asked.

"It's their nature," Rosaleth said. "They don't think like we do. No matter how much they look like us, they're definitely not human."

Across the wagon, Mistress Lirella announced, "I found it—the Treaty of Macomber. Witches may pass through the fey woods provided they do not tarry and provided they pay homage to the rulers of the woods as they pass. We'll need a suitable gift—I suggest one of the rarer herbs we purchase yesterday. The Briseis' Tears, perhaps."

Rosaleth groaned. "Of course it would be the most expensive one," she said. "After all that haggling, and I'm still going to have to find another one."

"We must all make sacrifices," said Mistress Eve loftily. "The rain's letting up—let's get going."

The rain had indeed lightened from a downpour to a grey drizzle. We all bundled up against the wet, and piled out of the Wagon. It was cramped to have all of us riding outside, but there was enough space with us girls sitting on the back edge of the wagon and the adults up front that we could make do. Lord Ebonfeather landed on Constance's shoulder and quorked unhappily. Secret and Starry trotted alongside us.

"At least we can spend more time with our familiars outside," Silke said, nuzzling Pipsie to her cheek fondly. I hadn't seen where the chipmunk had come from, but she was small enough that she could have been hiding herself anywhere. "It's not like Pipsie would make much of a mess inside."

"It's only fair that if the others can't go inside that I stay outside too, dearie," Pipsie said. *"It's not so bad when it's not raining like this."*

"I, for one, wonder at the direction we're heading," Lord Ebon-feather said. HIs voice was deep, commanding, and very proud. *"It seems to me that we make for the lands of the Fair Folk. Is that wise?"*

"They wouldn't be doing it if they didn't have a reason," Secret said. *"I'm sure they know what they're doing."* I was glad of my familiar's support, but I wished I shared her confidence.

We had been into the woods for only a short time before we caught our first glimpse of the fey. Small, winged figures darted around us, tittering and laughing, marvelling at the strangers in their midst. As we moved further into the forest, our impromptu entourage grew, adding more varieties of Fair Folk—small brown-clad figures kept pace running alongside us, small, bearded men in pointed caps peered out from the boles of hollow trees, and a few of the trees themselves uprooted and wandered after us. I felt like my eyes would pop out of my head if they grew any wider at the spectacle that accompanied us.

And then, abruptly, the chattering host fell silent. Rosaleth pulled up on the reins and the Wagon slowed and halted. "Girls," she said softly, "come on up here."

We hopped down from our perches on the back of the wagon and hurried to the front, where a path had been left open by the various Fair Folk who were our escort. A light shone from some-where, and a slender man in shining silver armor, riding the back of a magnificent white stag, emerged from behind the trees, accom-panied by a beautiful girl who looked no older than me, riding on a golden doe.

Mistress Lirella cleared her throat and spoke. "We bid you greetings, O gracious rulers of the Fair Folk. We are witches, trav-elling through these lands, and in accordance with the Treaty of Macomber we request passage unhindered. We have brought a gift in homage to you—this flowering plant of Briseis' Tears." Rosaleth passed forward the plant, a grimace on her face quickly concealed.

The man astride the stag simply nodded, but the girl slid off the deer and approached. "Such a lovely gift," she said, in a voice that reminded me of the pure tones of a silver flute being played. "We accept, of course, and in accordance with the ancient treaty we grant you passage." A small group of the winged Fair Folk gathered and collected the plant from Mistress Lirella. "But long has it been since civilized mortals set foot in these woods, and I would bid you tell us of the world outside. How fares the race of Man in these times?"

"Much the same as ever," Mistress Liraleth answered. She seemed to be acting as spokeswoman for our group, which was fine by me.

"Truly," said the girl. "A pity. Once, your people were mighty in magics and stood poised for greatness. Often I reflect on this with sadness and gladness both—sadness that a great people might be so diminished, but gladness that our two kinds did not come to war. For that would have been the inevitable outcome of things otherwise." She sighed sadly.

"But look, you have brought fledglings among us," she said then, sadness turning to delight in an instant. "And such pretty flowers they are. I see that they are but recently awakened to this world of magic, but already they must have an inkling of their potential." She walked in front of us, her eyes lingering on Constance as she spoke of potential.

"Tell me, young one," she said to Constance. "What will you do with the power you will one day command?"

Mistress Eve looked like she urgently wished to interrupt, but Mistress Alina and Rosaleth each took one of her arms, whispering in her ears, and she slumped back down.

"I..." Constance hesitated. "I do not know, great lady," she said finally.

"Ah, you have been schooled well," smiled the girl, with no malice in her voice. "Caution befits a young flower dealing with the Fair Folk." She turned to Sara next. "And you, little blossom, tell me, what would you do with the knowledge you will gain from your studies?"

"I will share it, of course." Sara set her jaw, and I was worried for a moment that the girl-Queen of the woods might be offended, but she simply laughed, a bright, clear sound. "An excellent answer. Your mistress is to be commended. And you, little bloom" this time, facing Silke, "what do you hope to see with the magics you will learn?"

"As much as I can," Silke whispered, then swallowed hard. I couldn't blame her nervousness—I knew I was next. The girl-Queen laughed again. "So careful," she said. "But Fair is fair." She came to stand in front of me, and regarded me silently for what seemed an endless moment before speaking. "You, little one—I would know your name."

"Tally," I said.

"Tally," she repeated, as though tasting the sound of my name. "I have no further question for you, Tally," she said, abruptly. "You are free to pass through these lands as you will, but meddle not, linger not." She turned, and her golden doe knelt to allow her to climb back onto its back.

"Farewell, young witches," she said. "I hope we meet again someday." And just as suddenly as they arrived, she and her armored companion departed. The noises of the assembled Fair Folk resumed slowly, and Rosaleth let out an explosive sigh.

"You did well, girls," she said.

We hurried through the remainder of the woods, though not so fast as to give the appearance of fleeing. When we were finally out, Constance turned to me asked the question I had been wondering since the girl-Queen of the Fair Folk had left:

"Why did she want to know your name, but nothing else? She asked the rest of us difficult questions." She wasn't happy that I had once again been singled out.

I shrugged helplessly. "I don't know," I said. "I was wondering that myself. Maybe she couldn't think of anything to ask?"

We both knew that wasn't it. There was some other reason behind the mystery, but I couldn't say what it was, and none of our mistresses had seen fit to explain. I resolved to ask Rosaleth about it later, but she was busy for the rest of the day and went to sleep immediately after dinner, leaving me to lay awake wondering late into the night.

Cottage

The next morning after breakfast—a simple, but quite tasty porridge, with small chunks of apple mixed in—Mistress Eve consulted a map she had produced from the Wagon's apparently quite useful library, joined by the other witches. I fidgeted while they plotted the course we'd taken through the fey woods, pulling out my fortune deck and shuffling through it, looking at the illustrations more than anything else.

"Well," Mistress Eve said, "it looks like if nothing else, that detour ended up saving us a day or so after all is said and done. I wouldn't have chosen it, but we're ahead of schedule now.

"I don't think any of us would have chosen the fey woods if we'd had a better option," Rosaleth said.

"I thought they were quite beautiful," Silke said, "but then it was a little scary when that girl asked us all questions."

"You did well," Mistress Alina said reassuringly. "The Queen is often mercurial, but it's their nature."

"She wanted us to slip up," said Constance. She shuddered. "I could tell she wanted me to say something she could use to manipulate me."

"The fey like to collect mortals with power," Mistress Eve said. "It's a way for them to show their superiority. Or just a game they play among each other. As I said, if we'd had any other choice, I would not have exposed you to them so soon in your training."

"On the plus side," Mistress Alina said, "We should be reaching our new homes today, rather than tomorrow."

"Our new homes?" Silke asked. "Will we not be staying together? I thought—well, since we've been together so far..."

"We can't do our duties if we just stay together," Mistress Alina said. "There's a small group of little villages that we'll be taking on—the witches who looked after them before have retired, and we're inheriting their cottages. We'll be close enough that it will be easy to visit. You'll get to see your friends, I promise, just not every day."

"Besides, we can always see if talking like this will work over longer distances," I said mentally, including Sara and—though I didn't really want to talk to her—Constance as well. It was only fair, after all—she was one of us, even if she could be insufferable sometimes.

We spent the day's travel largely engaged in small talk, the kind of conversation you have when you're going to have to say goodbye soon and don't want to think about it. A little bit after lunchtime the Wagon rolled to a stop. We peered outside and were surprised to see a strange looking building, ramshackle and with an odd, off-kilter second floor climbing into what almost appeared to be a small tower, with a crooked chimney on top. The front garden was overgrown with weeds, but I also saw some herbs I recognized growing as well, though nearly choked off by the unwanted plants.

"Ah," said Mistress Lirella, "quite nice. A little bit of cleanup and this shall do nicely."

"We're going to live *here*?" Sara asked, incredulous. "But it looks so...odd."

"Witches' dwellings usually do," Mistress Lirella said. "Do you remember what I told you about ley lines, Sara? That they are shaped by the environment around them? Witches often build their houses to shape the ley lines where they live into more advantageous configurations. The end result is an unusual aesthetic, but a usable nexus where the witch makes her home."

As she explained, I focused—as I was certain the other apprentices were doing as well—and saw she was correct. Though it was a bizarre house, there was indeed a nexus here, exactly as Mistress Lirella had said.

"It just looks like the roof leaks," Sara said.

Midnight and Starry seemed to like it well enough, though, stalking off into the garden to chase off any vermin that might have taken up residence. Sara collected her belongings—none of us had packed much, but Sara had a bag of books in addition to a few changes of clothes and personal effects—and brought them inside. Mistress Lirella likewise moved her belongings from the Wagon to the cottage, which took somewhat longer, since she had more to move. We all pitched in to help out.

The cottage didn't look too bad inside—the furniture was covered by sheets of cloth, and there was dust everywhere and cobwebs in the corners, but from what we could see, the roof did not in fact appear to leak. There was a rickety looking set of stairs up into the second floor, and another up to the third floor—really just a single small bedroom, with windows overlooking the grounds.

"Can I sleep here?" Sara asked.

Mistress Lirella smiled, and nodded. "If you like, my dear," she said.

We bade farewell to Sara and Mistress Lirella once they had been somewhat settled in.

"Don't forget us," Silke said to her.

"Don't worry," Sara replied. *"I strongly suspect we'll still see a lot of each other."*

I hugged Sara tightly. "That's a promise," I said.

We arrived at the next cottage a couple of hours later. This time, it looked much less likely to topple over in a strong wind, but instead was painted brightly and in clashing colors.

"Do the colors help with shaping the ley lines?" Silke asked dubiously.

"No." Mistress Alina sighed. "No, they don't."

"I think they're adorable," said Pipsie. *"It makes the cottage look very unique."*

It did that, certainly. Again, the inside was solid, but dusty and looked as though it had been unoccupied for some time. The kitchen, however, was the real treasure of the place—pots and pans of all shapes and sizes, and a wood stove in excellent condition, plus what appeared to be a well-stocked pantry of clearly labelled spices.

"I think I can cope," said Mistress Alina, on seeing the kitchen, "with having to get a new paint job, if it means that this kitchen is mine."

When I hugged Silke goodbye, she pressed a small cloth pouch into my hands. "Mints," she explained when I gave her a quizzical look. "For after you take your medicine."

I grinned and hugged her again, tighter.

While we rode towards the next cottage, the four of us who remained on the wagon—Mistress Eve, Constance, Rosaleth and myself—all rode up front. It was slightly cramped but less lonely than sitting in the back, especially with half of our number gone.

"If the cottages are built to shape the leylines into a nexus," Constance asked, "then doesn't that mean that someone could build something else, something that doesn't have to double as a living space, to more purposefully do that? Make a Grand Nexus, maybe, or something even greater?'

"It does," Mistress Eve said. She let out a long sigh. "Many of the Grand Nexus that exist today have structures to amplify them—stone circles, most often, or things of that sort. In the past, some tried to organize entire kingdoms with building projects to focus each leyline in the land into one Grand Nexus at the heart of the kingdom. It never ended well. Most of the time, there was a miscalculation somewhere and it simply didn't work right, but the stories of magical kingdoms lost in time, sealed away by walls of thorns forevermore are usually agreed to be based on cases where it did work."

"What could a witch do, in a Grand Nexus like that?" Constance asked, leaning forward.

"The power would be...almost impossible to comprehend," Mistress Eve said. "Certainly impossible to control. There are reasons we don't try to do such things anymore, Constance."

Constance leaned back, nodding. "I understand, Mistress," she said. "I was only asking to learn."

The next cottage came into view then. It was not particularly odd looking—just a squat stone building with a thatched roof. A young man was waiting by it, hat in hands, looking worried.

"You must be Mistress Eve," he said, as the Wagon rolled to a stop.

"I am," Mistress Eve said.

"Please, Mistress, I know you've only just got here, but it's my Da. He fell off the ladder while trying to repair our roof, and, well, please, I beg you to help him."

Rosaleth laid a hand on Eve's shoulder. "Go," she said. "I know what's yours in the wagon. Tally and I will bring your things in for you.

Mistress Eve nodded, though she did go into the wagon long enough to fetch a bag of herbs and tools that might be of use. Constance and I did not hug—we did pause to regard each other for a few moments. In the end, she nodded at me.

"Tally," she said.

"Constance," I said.

Then she went to join Mistress Eve, and the agitated young man.

It took Rosaleth and I a little bit longer to move their things into the cottage, without help from anyone else. This cottage seemed to be slightly cleaner than the others had been, and I commented to that effect to Rosaleth.

"It's been lived in more recently," she said. "Old Mother Desna was the last witch to retire out here."

"That makes sense," I said. "And our cottage is the last one, right?"

"Right," said Rosaleth. "I think that's everything. Shall we head on home, Tally?"

The sun was beginning to set when we arrived at the last cottage—our cottage. I peered from where I sat beside Rosaleth to get a good look at it. It was to my surprise that I realized that it wasn't just one building, but a small collection of buildings, laid out willy-nilly.

"You'll get your own little cottage, from the look of it, Tally," said Rosaleth. "And it looks like there's a greenhouse by the garden...yes, this is going to be perfect." I could see she was right about the greenhouse—which meant we could grow plants even into the fall and winter. And there was a chicken coop, too, though with Secret around I doubted we'd be keeping chickens. Sure enough, Secret immediately checked the coop, and emerged a moment later, disappointed.

"The snack-house is empty, Tally," she said. *"Are we going to keep chickens?"*

"You'll just scare them off all the time, or eat them." Rosaleth leapt down and started to unpack her things. I, of course, had only a couple of dresses from the hand-me-downs in the wagon, and my fortune cards, to bring inside. I looked inside the smaller out-building that Rosaleth had indicated, and found it to be a small bedroom with a night-table and oil lamp, and set my bag on the bed before going to help Rosaleth finish moving her things inside, including transferring several plants into the greenhouse.

"But not my Briseis' Tears," Rosaleth said, mournfully. "That still hurts."

"What do we do about the Wagon?" I asked, once we'd finished.

"It knows its way home," Rosaleth said, then smacked the lead horse on the rump. "Go on, then! Home with you!" The team started moving, slowly at first, but picking up speed, and soon enough was out of sight.

"So," Rosaleth said then. "We've got our work cut out for us getting everything cleaned up tomorrow and organized properly, but that's a task for tomorrow. Tonight, let's get an early bedtime, shall we?"

I nodded, suddenly feeling exhausted. It had been a long day, after all. I knew I'd miss my friends—even though we'd only known each other for a short time, I already felt close to Silke, and Sara of course had been a good friend since I could remember. It even felt strange for Constance to be missing, pain though she was.

Rosaleth rubbed my head, mussing my hair. "Don't worry, Tally. You'll see your friends again. Besides, I have a feeling you're going to really like it here. Now get some sleep."

"Good night," I said, and went to climb into my new bed. It was soft, and it was warm, and I quickly fell into a dreamless slumber.

Home

It took Rosaleth and I several days to fully clean out the cottage and outbuildings and get properly settled in. We started with the garden and the greenhouse—or intended to, at least, until we saw the state of the toolshed. Then we started there, and moved on to the garden and greenhouse once we'd cleared it out and found the spades and shovels we'd need to do a proper job of turning the earth, weeding, and planting our own plants in the cleared space. It took three days, and only after we had safely transferred them did we shift our attention indoors.

"We'll keep for a little while in unfinished surroundings, but these plants need room to grow right away," Rosaleth had said.

It took us another day and a half to finish dusting and airing out the main cottage. The furniture proved to be worn but very comfortable, once uncovered from the sheets, and the kitchen, while less well-stocked than Mistress Alina's, was nevertheless supplied with all of the cooking implements we would reasonably need, though again, somewhat worn.

While much of the work was monotonous, I passed the time in conversation, sometimes with Rosaleth, more often with my fellow apprentices—even Constance joined in without too much malice in my direction, though she had regained some of her previous haughtiness.

The chicken coop, we decided, we would leave empty, as we would the goat pen, for the time being.

"I'm not that good at taking care of animals," Rosaleth said.

"Especially your long-suffering familiar," Snickers said, teasing her.

"Hush or I'll forget not to hide your favorite toy where you can't find it," Rosaleth said.

"A challenge," said Snickers, *"Please!"*

"You're impossible." Rosaleth laughed.

"You wouldn't have to take care of them for long," suggested Secret, licking her chops.

"Don't you start too," I said. I wasn't really upset, though. I already loved Secret as though she'd been by my side for years, and she knew it.

We had finished with the cleaning for little more than an hour before the first of the villagers from Greenwater, the nearby hamlet that was now under our care, came to visit us. The man introduced himself as Gulver, the foremost of the local farmers.

"We don't have much need for a proper mayor or anything like that," he said by way of explanation. "Most times, folk look to me for a cool head and a sensible decision, probably because I haven't steered them wrong yet. Listen, I had a nice whip-round when we heard word you'd moved in, brought you out some supplies from the folk in town. They'll be happy to know the old place is occupied again, and I'm sure glad myself to know that we can feel safer with you out here. Why, we've been danged lucky nobody's come down sick with worse than the sniffles since the place has been empty, but you'll find us a pretty healthy place." He cleared his throat, then, and awkwardly took his leave.

"It was nice of Gulver to bring us supplies like that," I said later, as we finished putting away the stocks he'd brought us of food and spices.

"It's so that we won't have to go into town. He'll be by every week—he's the most important man in town, so it falls to him to do it, probably. We'll get other visits here and there, too, from the folks who are sick, or want something from us, but otherwise they'll donate whatever they have to so that we won't have to come into town. So that we won't come into town." Rosaleth spoke matter-of-factly.

"Why?" I asked. It was all I could think of to say to that.

"We're the ones they call when someone gets sick, badly sick, or when there's a difficult birth, or someone gets hurt doing something foolish. When they don't get better, or the baby doesn't make it, or we have to take the leg off, it's what they remember—they don't blame us, but they don't want us around, either." Rosaleth turned to look me in the eye. "I did tell you you'd be an outcast," she said.

My friends later confirmed that they, too, had faced the same reception from the folk of their local villages, one and all.

"I went into town to go introduce myself to the local dressmaker, and the woman all but raced to get my measurements taken and then practically shoved me out the door!" said Constance. *"Mistress Eve said that I had to go back and explain that I didn't want her to make me a free dress—as if the only reason I would go into the shop was that I needed something!"*

"What did the dressmaker say?" I asked, morbidly interested despite myself—trust Constance to make the conversation about clothes, somehow.

"Well she apologized and said she hadn't realized that I had just been in for a social visit, since she's normally so busy that she doesn't have time to socialize, and that she would be happy to make a dress any time I did need one," Constance said. *"It's just like you said, anyway. I'm glad to see that Tally the Trickster isn't so special all the time, at least!"* Her tone was jovial, as if she were just teasing, but her words still carried some bite.

"Tally the Trickster?" Sara asked, and I wished I could give her a hug—her tone spoke volumes of what she thought of Constance's 'joke'.

I didn't want to get into a fight just then, though, so I said, *"Well, it is my favorite fortune card, after all, so it sorta fits. And it's alliterative!"* I winced, certain that that last would get me teased.

"I can think of something that's alliterative with Constance,' Sara's voice had the slightly clearer tone that told me she was 'speaking' only to me.

I snorted a laugh, but sent back *"Please don't."*

But it was too late—Tally the Trickster was my nickname from then on.

The days settled into a simple routine fairly quickly. We spent the mornings on housekeeping and chores - Rosaleth assigned me to maintaining the garden and greenhouse, while she would handle cooking meals and keeping the cottage from getting too dusty. Then, over lunch and into the afternoon, she would teach me lessons—usually simple magical theory, at least for the time being.

"You're already at least somewhat competent in herbalism, at least on an intellectual level—you've got a way to go on getting up to speed on preparation of the herbs in the first place for maximum efficacy, but that's why you're in the garden." Rosaleth had enumerated the reasoning behind the focus and direction of my studies early on. "Magic, you can't really learn on your own, and it isn't something that's entirely safe to experiment with unsupervised."

I thought of the fact that we still hadn't told anyone that we'd figured out mental speech and felt slightly guilty—but it seemed as though my fellow apprentices and I were delaying further every time the subject came up, which was admittedly less and less often as time wore on.

In the later afternoon, I normally spent time reading—the cottage had a small but highly focused collection of books on subjects of interest to witches. Rosaleth encouraged me to choose one or two topics to begin with, rather than try to absorb everything at once. Since she gave me free reign on choosing, I decided to learn more about the Fair Folk, and on seeing that the cabin's previous owner had left behind a slim tome on the subject of the fortune cards, my choice of second topic became obvious.

In the evenings, after we had eaten dinner and it had grown too dark to continue reading easily, Rosaleth would question me on the topics I was studying and on the subject of the day's lesson. At first I was bad at answering these impromptu quizzes, since every question I answered drove Rosaleth to ask a deeper, more difficult question, but as I grew to expect this pattern of questioning I also grew to understand the types of detail Rosaleth wanted me to focus on in my studies. Once that happened, I started to be able to pick those details out and make mental note of them. The first time I successfully answered all of Rosaleth's questions regarding the day's study, she rewarded me with a grin, a wink, and a battery of questions about the day before. Soon her questions ranged the entire time we'd been studying.

"No point in learning it if you're just going to let it go," she said. I remembered her telling me that she wasn't much of a teacher, but I wasn't so sure if she was as bad as she thought herself to be. I couldn't deny that I was learning a lot, and if much of it was self-study, that didn't mean it wasn't effective when coupled with her quizzes.

Eventually Rosaleth would be satisfied with my demonstration of understanding and I'd return to my smaller cabin, where I'd either practice with the fortune cards or write home to my family. I'd got a letter or two from Shalla and Uncle Grim—Gulver brought them up with the weekly supplies—before I realized that I had been here for just under a month—had been a girl and an apprentice witch for a full month.

I told Rosaleth the next morning, and after a moment of sur-prised reflection, she slowly grinned at me. "So you have!" she said. "Congratulations, Tally! How do you feel?"

"I feel...more comfortable here than I ever did back home," I answered. "I guess I feel like this is home now, even though I still love Uncle Grim and Shalla and miss them. And...I feel like I'm someone I actually like being, instead of dreading every day not feeling like I'm who I am." It was hard to put it into words, but Rosaleth seemed to understand what I meant well enough.

"I think you're going to find that things may get more confusing for you," she said. "That potion I made you doesn't work all at once—but you're going to start noticing some changes to your body soon, and trust me, they can be very confusing to experience for any girl."

"Well," I said, "I can't imagine they're going to be any more confusing than waking up in a body that doesn't feel like it belongs to you." I felt a surge of doubt, though, at the way Rosaleth raised her eyebrow at that.

"You'll see what I mean," she said with a glint of mischief in her eye. "I expect before the end of the week, in fact." She held up a letter Gulver had brought by. "We're going to have guests," she said.

Guests

The letter, Rosaleth explained, was from a friend of hers who spent most of his time wandering, but who was in the area and would be stopping by for a few days to visit and catch up.

"Will I have to give up my room?" I asked, nervous that Rosaleth would make me sleep on the sofa in the main cottage to give her guest a room to stay in.

"Oh Tally," she said, "I'm not going to do that to you. Don't worry, we'll sort out sleeping arrangements that work for everyone."

I was working in the garden, tending to the herbs that we would be sending to Shalla and Uncle Grim to make her medicine, when the guests arrived. I crouched down in the greenhouse a little bit when I saw them, more than a little intimidated.

The first guest was a tall, imposing man in a greatcoat. He carried a musket slung across his back and a short sword at his hip, and wore a broad-rimmed hat, weathered and beaten. His skin was tan and weathered, and he looked competent and tough.

The second, younger, shorter, was also dressed in a greatcoat—it seemed to fit him significantly less well. He also carried a musket, though he did not have any other visible weapons, and his face was tan, but lacked the grizzled weathering of his companion. He looked more curious than anything else.

The first man looked right at me, despite my half-hearted attempt at hiding myself, and strode towards me.

"Greetings, little lady," he said. "Is this Mistress Rosaleth's cottage, by any chance?"

I managed a squeak in response. Fortunately, I was spared further indignity by Rosaleth, appearing from the door of the cottage and rushing over to catch the terrifying man in an embrace.

"Val," she said, "you're frightening my apprentice."

"Thought you said you weren't going to take an apprentice," said the man—Val, I supposed. "Wasn't sure I was in the right place. Besides, I was being polite and friendly," he said, sounding a little hurt.

"She's twelve, Val, and you're in your full kit. Any sensible twelve year old girl would be terrified of you. Actually, the only reason I'm not is that I know what a big ol' softie you are." She nudged him in the side, and he winced.

"Sorry, Rose," he said. A pet name? Rosaleth didn't object to it, anyway.

"You're hurt, aren't you," she said, sternly.

"It's nothing," Val protested. "I got a bit sliced up fighting my last mark. Stitched it up already just fine."

"I've seen your needlework before, Val," Rosaleth said. "Inside, and I'll take a look at it."

"Now Rose—" he said, but she cut him off with a stern look, pointing to the cottage.

"Inside!" she repeated.

Sighing, he tipped his hat to me. "Little lady," he said, then slipped his musket off his back and passed it to the young man who accompanied him, who accepted it wordlessly.

I soon found myself left standing in awkward silence next to the young man.

"So," I said.

"So," he said.

We stood in silence a few more moments.

"I'm Tally," I said, when it was obvious that neither of us really knew what to say. "I'm Mistress Rosaleth's apprentice."

"Oh, I'm, ah, pleased to make your acquaintance," said the boy, awkwardly trying to juggle both muskets he was holding onto to give himself a free hand to extend. Finally he laid them against the wall of the greenhouse carefully and, wiping his hand on his greatcoat, offered it out to me. "My name is Simon, and I'm Master Valiant's apprentice. Assistant."

From inside the cottage, Val's voice roared in pain. Simon cringed.

"Don't be so melodramatic," I heard Rosaleth say. "That was going to get infected if you had left it like that. I don't know how you thought I wouldn't notice it, either. Now sit there nicely and keep pressure on it." She emerged from the cottage briskly, and listed off half a dozen herbs she needed me to bring her.

"Is your mistress always like that? So, intense, I mean?" Simon asked as I moved quickly to cut sprigs here and there, careful not to do anything to permanently damage the plants.

"She's just focused on doing the things that she knows need to be done first" I said. "We planted this garden before we properly settled into the cottage. Besides, your master comes off as pretty intense too," I said, heading to the cottage to give Rosaleth the herbs she'd requested. Inside, Val—Master Valiant?—sat shirtless on the couch, holding a wad of once-clean linen cloth to a wound in his side, one that appeared to be bleeding profusely, judging by the color of the linen.

"Thank you, Tally," Rosaleth said, then followed my gaze to Master Valiant. "Perhaps you should show Val's apprentice around while I take care of him," she suggested.

"Y-yes," I said. "I'll—yes."

I beat a hasty retreat, and beckoned for Simon to follow me.

"Well, Master Valiant is a monster hunter," Simon said, and it took me a moment to realize he was responding to my comment about how intense he was. "It's sort of a natural consequence, I guess. I'm going to be a monster hunter too, or, I guess, I am one, I mean, an apprentice," he said. "I saved Master Valiant's life, actually," he continued proudly. "That injury, he got it fighting a wild wyvern. Just a bladetail wyvern, mind, which was lucky, since they don't have venom like other breeds. Anyway, it had pounced on Master Valiant after it slashed him open like that, and then— BAM—I shot it off him. He says I'm a natural with the rifle, anyway."

"He likes you," Secret said from the shade nearby where she was comfortably seated, observing. *"He wants you to be impressed."*

I did my best to ignore Secret—I could see that Simon couldn't hear her.

"That seems like it would be a good talent for a monster hunter," I said.

"Well, it's only part of the job," Simon said, bolstered by my response. "I still have to learn a lot of things, like swordplay and beast lore, and Master Valiant says there's some tricks of magic that a true monster hunter uses—that's, um, part of why we're here. He said that we should always be on good terms with witches, and be friends with at least one witch. Um."

"He likes you," Secret repeated. *"He wants to ask you to be his friend now!"*

"Shh." I shushed her as subtly as I could.

"Would yo—huh?" he asked.

"Not you, sorry," I said. "My familiar is teasing me."

"Your familiar? Oh, I think I heard something about that—you have a magical companion animal, right?" He looked around and saw Secret, who winked at him.

"It's all right, Tally," Secret said. *"I don't mind if you like him."*

"Stop that!" I said to Secret, feeling a blush spreading on my face. "It's not—" I glanced at Simon and switched to mental speech. *"It's not like that for humans,"* I said. *"I only just met him."*

"But you think he's interesting," Secret said. *"And I can tell you don't mind him standing so close to you."*

I took a half-step away from Simon, who looked confused.

"She's saying...well, she's saying some things I'd rather not talk about. Um, so, you're going to be learning a lot too, then?"

Simon nodded. "I'm looking forward to learning about the different kinds of beasts and creatures out there more than I am to learning swordplay,' he said. "I had this book when I was little, a bestiary, with pictures and stories about all of the magical animals, and I just...really wanted to see them."

"Why become a hunter, then? I mean, doesn't that mean you have to kill them?" I asked.

"Not always," Simon said. "We only do that when we have to. Sometimes the things we hunt are smart, and we can talk to them, and find out why they're angry and hurting people. Sometimes we can trap them and move them somewhere else, somewhere safer for them and for people. We only kill things when there's no other way, at least, that's what Master Valiant teaches me." He kicked at the ground, a little bitterly. "It's not always that way, though, with other hunters."

"Oh," I said.

"How about you? What sorts of things do you learn about? Plants, and healing, I guess, because I saw you working in the garden and your Mistress Rosaleth went right to tending to Master Valiant. But that can't be all."

I glanced at him, impressed by his observant nature. I felt a little strange talking to him—this was the longest conversation I'd ever had with a boy, even from before. Most of the time I had nothing in common with them, but Simon seemed observant, thoughtful, cute, and clever.

Wait. Cute? Where had that come from? I decided I would have to have a talk with Secret later about teasing me that way. She was putting weird thoughts into my head.

"I am also learning about magic," I said, trying to keep my mind on the topic at hand, "and about the Fair Folk, and also how to read fortune cards."

"Fortune cards?" Simon asked, surprised. "I thought witches didn't put much stock into things like that. Not," he hastened to add, "that I know much about witches."

"It depends on the witch, apparently," I said. "I came into a set of the cards, so I decided it would make sense to learn to read them." A sudden impulse came over me. "Would you like me to read your fortune?" I asked.

"I would be honored, Mistress Tally" said Simon. I felt the blush again.

"You can just call me Tally," I said.

Simon

I quickly fetched my fortune cards and a cloth to lay them on from my room—I was certainly not comfortable with the idea of inviting a strange boy into my room, even if he was polite and seemed nice. I glanced around and settled on laying the cloth out across the old, scarred stump we used to chop firewood. I fetched a couple of empty flower-pots and turned them upside down to make makeshift seats for us by the improvised table. Simon sat opposite me, looking impressed by my resourcefulness. Secret deigned to saunter over, sitting herself to one side, where she could watch the proceedings with a clear view of everything.

"Shuffle these, please, while thinking of the question you'd like answered," I said, sliding the deck towards him. "But don't say your question aloud. Just focus on it."

I tried to focus on the flow of energy along the ley lines while he obligingly shuffled, the way the book I was learning from suggested. This would be the first time I performed a reading for someone else, and that made me feel very self-conscious—which of course made it a bit difficult to stay focused.

"You're turning red again, Tally," Secret said. I ignored her.

"I'm done shuffling," Simon said. He passed the cards back to me.

I laid out the three cards face down, in the same spread the old fortune teller who had given me the cards had used. I had learned several of the more complicated spreads that Mistress Lirella had mentioned, but I did not feel nearly confident enough to perform my first ever reading for someone else—someone I'd just met— with anything more complicated than the very basics.

I took a deep breath, and turned over the first card. It was *The Beast*, a card bearing the image of a strange and ugly creature made from parts of several normal animals. The strange creature pursued a fleeing figure. "The first card is your past," I said. "It shows something about what brought you to where you stand now, in regards to your situation. The Beast can be a sign of violence, or of being made to leave somewhere against your will, or it can mean a literal beast of some kind. Um."

Simon looked rapt, so far. I guessed my interpretation wasn't too far from what he was expecting, because he simply nodded at me to continue, eyes intent.

"The second card represents your current situation as it pertains to your question" I said, turning it over to reveal *The Tome*. The card depicted a large, ornately bound book, laid open to show a page of arcane-looking writing and diagrams. "The Tome represents learning and knowledge, but also secrets and magic. It can indicate that you want to learn something, or that magic is in some way involved with your question. Is this...making sense, so far?" I asked.

"Yes," said Simon, "It does make sense. You seem a little bit nervous, but I don't think you should be. You're good at this."

I felt my cheeks redden again—which Secret confirmed a moment later. *"I think you want to impress him, too, don't you?"* she asked. I continued to studiously ignore her, reaching instead for the third and final card.

I jerked my hand back in surprise. It was The Trickster, the beautiful image of the fox staring back at me.

"Are you all right?" Simon asked, half-rising in concern. "What does it mean?"

"I'm—I'm fine," I said, managing to keep my voice even. "It's nothing bad. I just—it's nothing." I didn't want to explain my sense of personal connection to this card, or that my friends had taken to calling me Tally the Trickster, so, despite Simon's continued look of concern, I pressed on. "The Trickster is someone who..." *subverts fate*, I did not say. "Who doesn't always do things the way other people expect. They are an actor for change, who can overturn the way things are by their actions. When the card represents a person..." I paused.

"Tally?" Simon asked as the pause stretched on.

"Sorry, I had to try to remember what it meant," I lied. "When it represents a person it can be anyone, and often the last person you expect."

Or me. The Trickster could represent me.

"I still think I smell better," Secret said.

"Thank you, Tally," Simon said. "That was very helpful, and definitely more meaningful than I expected—you know what I mean, right? All those stories about these cards just being a con? Not to suggest that you're—"

"I see you've trained your apprentice well in the fine tradition of putting his foot in his mouth," Rosaleth said from nearby—we had both missed the approach of our respective teachers.

"He's never demonstrated his gift for it so eloquently before," Master Valiant said, fondly rustling Simon's hair. "I can't hardly blame the lad, though, talking to such a pretty girl. You cut us off before we could properly introduce everyone, Rose," he said.

"You were hurt, and you're no good at patching yourself up," Rosaleth said. "This is my apprentice, Tally. Tally, this is my, ah, friend, Valiant."

Master Valiant tipped his hat toward me as he had before. "A pleasure to meet you, Tally," he said. "Simon, this is Mistress Rosaleth, my friend. Rose, this is my apprentice, Simon."

Simon bowed to Rosaleth. "I'm honored to meet you, Mistress Rosaleth," he said.

"Rosaleth is fine," she said. "And you've already met each other, I assume. My apologies for such an out-of-order introduction."

"I'm still a little surprised you took an apprentice, Rose," Master Valiant said. "It's clear enough you've chosen well, of course, and meaning no disrespect to you, Tally, of course. But you always said you weren't the sort to take apprentices."

Rosaleth shrugged. "When an apprentice as good as Tally falls into your lap," she said, "you don't let the opportunity pass by."

"Um, please excuse me for a few moments," I said. "I'd like to go put away my fortune cards now."

"Was it a good reading?" Rosaleth asked Simon. "Did she answer your question for you?"

"Oh, yes," he said. "It was very meaningful!"

"It definitely doesn't mean anything," Sara said, not long after. I had, as soon as I had got into my room, hurriedly contacted my friends and explained what had happened during the reading.

"You don't even know what he was asking about, Tally," Silke reassured me. *"It was probably some hunter thing about how to safely hunt monsters. You said his master had been hurt, right? The Beast means the monster who hurt his master, The Tome is about learning, and The Trickster is what he needs to learn to be—cunning*

and clever. Simple!" Silke had been briefly upset that she hadn't got to be the first person to have her fortune told by me, and I'd had to promise to give her a full, detailed reading the next time we saw each other to satisfy her.

"Well he certainly wouldn't be asking about you, anyway," Constance the Cruel said. When Tally the Trickster had stuck, Sara had privately started referring to her with that nickname, and I couldn't help but feel it fit sometimes. Constance waited just long enough for the barb to sink in before adding, *"You just met him what, twenty minutes ago? He hasn't known you long enough to be asking you to read his fortune about you."* It wasn't that she was right that bothered me, it was the way she put it—always looking for those little ways to get in her jabs.

"Is he cute, then? You have to tell us if he's cute," Silke said.

I was saved—as usual—by Sara. *"Tally doesn't have to tell us anything, if she doesn't want to. She's already flustered. Tally, I'm sure it means nothing—but you shouldn't be talking to us if you've got guests. Everything will be fine. Go on back before you're missed."*

Sara was, as ever, the sensible one. I said a hurried goodbye to the others and quickly stepped back outside, nearly bumping into Rosaleth.

"I was just coming to see if you'd got lost," she said, winking at me. "Are you all right?"

"Yes, I just..." I just what? "...can't come up with an excuse that you're going to believe after a pause like that," I said lamely.

"How well you know me, my little apprentice." Rosaleth laughed. "What's eating you?" She followed my gaze. "Ah," she said.

"I didn't say anything," I said. It was a weak protest even to my ears.

"You don't have to. He's cute, and you're at the right age to be noticing boys. I did try to warn you that things would get confusing," she said.

"But I thought you meant...I guess I didn't realize that was what you meant."

"Don't worry, Tally," she said, hugging me. "It's normal to feel things around cute boys. I wasn't much older than you when I met Val, actually. I know I don't need to tell you this, but don't rush into anything serious."

"Because I'm still...you know...?" I asked, feeling a little hurt. "You're right, you don't need to tell me that."

"No, my little Tally, that's not why at all. That matters much less than you think, if you're with the right person. And besides, you won't have to worry about that forever. This is actually already a good sign. No, I want you not to rush in because you've got plenty of time. Val and I had been sweethearts for a good couple of years before we got really serious."

I gaped. "You and Master Valiant are—"

"Lovers," she said simply. "It's not actually all that uncommon for witches to have relationships, Tally. I'm probably not the best role model for this particular situation, but I also don't think you're the kind of girl who doesn't know how to be careful. And I suspect you could do worse than young Simon over there. Who, by the way, will be staying for awhile, so that I can make sure that Val doesn't reopen that wound or do something else stupid before he's properly healed, so if you actually do want to pursue him you'll get your chance."

"I told you, Mistress Rosaleth" Secret said, nuzzling at my legs. *"She keeps turning red. See?"*

I groaned, but inside a part of me did a little dance of excitement. Simon and Valiant staying here meant a number of changes, for certain, and it was definitely going to be awkward around Simon until I figured out whether I wanted to pursue him. Did he even like me? Secret said he did. And he was cute. Maybe it wouldn't be so bad to be someone's sweetheart.

I was definitely not telling Constance about any of this, though.

Definitely not.

Training

The next few days saw a change to the routine that had been established in my life, for obvious reasons. While I continued to work in the garden in the mornings, Valiant and Simon quickly converted our goat pen into a small training area, with a simple dummy erected for Simon to practice with a wooden training sword against.

"I don't understand," said Simon, drenched in sweat after one particularly vigorous workout, "why I'm practicing to use a sword against a human dummy."

"Two reasons. First, I want you to be able to handle a sword properly in whatever situation you're in, and that means starting with the basics." Valiant drummed a finger against his palm, adding a second finger as he continued. "Second, not all monsters come in monstrous forms. You know that."

Simon seemed to think about that for a few moments, then nodded and went back to his practice.

I wondered if that had anything to do with the question he had asked when I read his fortune, but it seemed like a very personal thing to ask and I didn't want to offend Simon, so I let it be. It wasn't as though I had nothing in my past I didn't want to talk about, after all, so I could easily see how that line of questioning might end the friendship we had started to develop.

I still hadn't decided yet what to do about the way my tummy felt when I looked at Simon, but it didn't seem like he disliked me, and Secret continued helpfully advising me that she was certain he was interested in making a good impression with me.

"This is all much easier for foxes," she said. *"I don't know why humans don't just say how you feel about each other and then be done with all this waffling about."*

"I don't really know how I feel yet," I said. I hugged her, which she seemed to enjoy—in small doses, anyway. "It's confusing for me, too."

Rosaleth's daily lessons were expanded to include Simon, and shifted a little in topic to include subjects more relevant to the pursuit of monster hunting. I learned about the various types of wyverns, which ones were venomous and which ones were not. I learned about manticores, which didn't often appear in our cold climate, and about chimeras, which didn't care about the weather and might make a nest anywhere they could find good hunting. Rosaleth also told us about some of the more human-shaped beings classified as monsters—vampires, werewolves, and even ghosts— who could be the most dangerous of all, as they could possess an innocent person and make them appear to be monstrous, all the while hiding their own presence.

"But the stories always talk about how evil vampires are," I said when that topic arose. "How can ghosts be worse?"

"Vampires are dangerous, very much so, but they're also re- stricted in many ways. They can't go out in the daylight, they must feed—leaving telltale marks on their victims—and they must spend each day sleeping in the soil of their homeland. They can control and warp minds, but not as invisibly as ghosts can. Most surviv- ing vampires have done so by making arrangements and treaties, similar to the Fair Folk, that they will limit their hunting and abide by strict rules, in exchange for being left alone in their domains. It's not a situation that anyone really likes, but they're civilized monsters, and can be bargained with."

Werewolves, on the other hand, had no self control, and while they were usually aware of their monthly transformations, they had no memory of the actions their beast-selves might have taken while in human form. Fortunately, while there was no cure, there were ways that a werewolf could be contained.

"It's not a great life," Valiant explained—having witnessed first- hand at least one werewolf who struggled against their curse. "They chain themselves and lock themselves in cages during the full moon, to keep themselves from harming innocents. If the cage should ever fail, they know that there will certainly be blood on their hands by the dawn, because the beast hates to be chained. But some try it anyway, and as long as they're careful to make sure the chains aren't weakening and the cage isn't ever left unlocked, they can live. The alternative, well, it's not very easy for most to face their own deaths. Some hunters don't offer the choice, either, arguing that it's inevitable that the chains and the cage will eventually fail, so don't expect a werewolf to give you a warm welcome even if they hate what they've become."

Other lessons were not so depressing, though. We learned about unicorns, and their attraction to purity. Sometimes a unicorn would wander into human lands, and monster hunters would herd them away from more mundane hunters, who prized them as trophies. We learned about the noble griffin, and its relative, the hippogriff—both creatures capable of great savagery when angered, but who would sometimes respond to noble and honorable humans by deigning to allow them to ride on their backs. Winged horses, slightly more common but far more skittish, would also sometimes allow humans to ride them, and all three types of creature were said to be extremely loyal once their trust had been won.

In addition to Simon joining into Rosaleth's lessons, Rosaleth asked me to share with him what I was learning about the Fair Folk. At first I protested, since I didn't feel like I had mastered the material myself, but Rosaleth insisted it would be a good opportunity for me to review it. While I privately worried that I would have a hard time staying focused being largely left alone with Simon, he proved to be a quick study, and despite a bit of awkwardness, we were able to stay on task.

Together, we reviewed the basic rules of dealing with the Fair Folk, and the dangers of not adhering to the letter of any bargain with them, as well as the dangers of assuming that they would adhere to anything beyond the letter of any agreement they made. We learned the names for the different types of Fair Folk, from the winged pixies to the wizened gnomes, the playful fauns to the beautiful dryads, and the imposing treants—all of which I had witnessed firsthand during our journey.

"Are they really so dangerous?" Simon asked me. "What I mean to say is, you said you came through their woods, and nobody was hurt or anything."

"It wasn't so simple as that," I said. "It seemed like a magical experience at the time, but I could tell that the grown-up witches were all very nervous, and they nearly panicked when the Queen started asking us questions."

"You met the Queen of the Fair Folk?" he asked, leaning forward. I felt my tummy do a flip, but managed not to blush.

"We did," I said. "She looked about our age, and she rode a golden doe. She laughed a lot, and very prettily, but she looked at us and saw right to the core of what we were, and she asked us all questions. Well, all but me—she only asked my name."

"What kinds of questions?" Simon asked. "And why would she only ask for your name?"

"She asked Constance what she would do with her power, and she asked Sara what she would do with her knowledge—that kind of thing. I don't know why she didn't ask me anything but my name, though." I had spent a lot of time wondering that, but still hadn't come up with a satisfactory answer. "Constance was annoyed by it, though. She seems to think I somehow feel like I'm more special than anyone else."

"But you are special," Simon said, and this time I did blush. I noticed that he had the good grace to be blushing as well. "I mean, you're—you're a witch's apprentice, so of course you're special, but you're also smart and funny and...and I'm just showing off my gift for putting my foot in my mouth, as Master Valiant would say."

I felt the blush on my cheeks deepen, and wished I had learned a spell to turn myself invisible.

"I...Tally, I'm sorry, I didn't mean to say that that was the only reason you're special. I'm...not great with words, sometimes. Um. I think you're very wonderful, and I just...I wanted you to know that. And I'll go away now, because I've gone and embarrassed you terribly." He rose to leave.

"Don't," I said, my voice soft. "Don't go."

Simon sat, looking abashed but hopeful.

"I have to tell you something," I said, swallowing hard. I'd been mulling over what I would do if he ever did or said something like this, and I'd decided that the only way forward was total honesty. It might hurt, and it might change things forever, but I didn't want him not to understand.

"Okay," he said.

"I'm...not like other girls you've probably known," I said. "I mean, I am in some ways, most ways even, but, I..." I struggled to find the words I needed. "I wasn't always. I have to take a potion every day—you've seen it, right?"

He nodded, not speaking.

"That potion is so that I can be like other girls. I...I'm not sure how to say it."

"You don't have to, Tally." Simon's brown eyes were intense, and serious. "I'm not sure exactly what's different about you, but it's part of what makes you who you are, and that's the person I...the person I like." And then we were both blushing again. "So, if it's part of who you are, then I don't mind, okay?"

I managed to nod.

"Finally," Secret said. *"I was beginning to worry the pair of you would never admit it to each other."*

Simon nearly jumped. "Who—who said that?" he demanded, surprised.

"That's Secret," I said. "My familiar. I didn't think you could hear her, until just now."

"Well I was hardly going to talk to him if you didn't know how you felt," Secret said, a trifle indignant. *"I didn't want to scare him off, after all."*

Simon looked at me again with those brown eyes. "You've felt this way too, then?" he asked.

I nodded again. "That's what I was trying to say, yes," I said. "I was worried that you wouldn't like me if you found out I was different."

"I like you because you're different", he declared. "Tally, may I hug you?"

I nodded. The hug felt like the best thing in the whole world.

Winter

Master Valiant's convalescence seemed to stretch on over several weeks, as Rosaleth did not seem inclined to give him a clean bill of health until he was fully healed. Valiant protested periodically about the delay, but never seemed to do so particularly strenuously.

"You let that wound get infected once already," Rosaleth said. "I'm not letting you out of my sight till you're fully healed."

Neither Valiant nor Simon seemed to be particularly bothered by staying, though—and neither Rosaleth nor I minded their presence. Gulver the farmer seemed to be somewhat perplexed by their continued stay, but raised no complaint, simply adjusted the amount of supplies he brought out weekly to account for them. He seemed slightly friendlier to Valiant than to Rosaleth and I, inviting him to come down to the tavern for a drink and a tale of old hunts sometime, but Valiant politely refused, and Gulver didn't press the issue.

We had still not really made many connections with the villagers, despite the weeks we'd dwelled in close proximity. Gulver assured us weekly that everyone was in good health in the village, and there were no problems that needed the attention of a witch, and while we'd had occasional visits from other villagers with assorted minor aches and pains, Rosaleth typically sent them off with willow-bark tea and a bit of friendly advice. They seemed grateful, and most had sent small gifts in thanks, but we were still clearly outsiders.

The first snowfall arrived two weeks into Valiant and Simon's stay, and when it did, it came fearsomely, with a storm that lasted almost a day and a half.

"I suppose we'll wait out the winter here, if you'll have us," said Valiant thoughtfully. "Looks like it'll be a rough one, and I don't much relish roughing it if it's going to be this bad."

"You know you're more than welcome," said Rosaleth. "It's going to be a little cramped, but having a big, strong, manly man around to help us shovel all this snow will be helpful."

Valiant clutched at his side, making a face. "My injury may keep me from such strenuous work," he said. "Fortunately, my apprentice could use the workout."

Simon had the good sense not to object.

Later that evening, I was helping Simon apply a salve I had made for sore muscles while he had been out shovelling snow, when suddenly the cabin was filled by the sound of pounding on the door.

"Mistress Rosaleth, please help!" Gulver's voice sounded, muffled by the door and the snow outside. Valiant opened the door and bustled the man into the cabin.

"It's my daughter," Gulver explained, clearly distraught. "She's with child, and the midwife was to be back in time for the birth, but—" He choked.

"The snow's cut her off, and your daughter's child is coming earlier than expected," Rosaleth finished, standing up and gathering her heavy winter clothing. "Tally, get ready—we're going at once."

Hurriedly, I pulled on my cloak and mittens, pulling up the hood. Rosaleth gathered a small bag of supplies and nodded to Gulver.

"Let's go," she said.

The path to town was heavy with snow, and only Gulver's stamped-down passage made it any easier to get through. I followed after Gulver and Rosaleth, and still found myself struggling to wade after them. Secret leaped along after me—though I didn't see Snickers around. Rosaleth's familiar had complained a great deal about the snow already, and presumably had stayed in where it was warm. Though the storm had let up somewhat, it was still too cold and windy for us to have much in the way of conversation along the way. We trudged down into the village. I had to admit it was picturesque, largely covered in undisturbed snow—it was a smaller village than I had grown up in, but still similar enough to feel homely.

Gulver's house was the largest one in town—it was clear he was indeed the foremost of the townsfolk. He opened the door and held it for Rosaleth and I to come inside. Secret darted in alongside me. Gulver opened his mouth as if to protest, but decided against it.

"This is a bigger den than the one you have," Secret said.

"He's got a big family, from the sounds of it" I answered silently.

That proved true—in addition to the pregnant daughter and her husband, there were two younger girls, a little older than myself, and a young man who looked like Gulver must have twenty years previous, and a worried looking older woman who I took to be Gulver's wife. All of them were surrounding the bedside of the daughter who was giving birth, offering support and encouragement.

Rosaleth took charge immediately. The two girls were sent off to fetch clean cloth and boil water, the brother sent to fetch firewood. I was tasked with being a second set of hands for Rosaleth, and did my best to act calmly and reassuringly, as much for the benefit of the worried family members as anyone else.

An hour or so later, the newborn babe was sleeping in his mother's arms, both safe and healthy. Rosaleth and I had withdrawn to the kitchen to give the family some privacy, and we were both busily scrubbing our hands. Rosaleth gave me an appraising look.

"You did well," she said, "but I get the feeling that was your first time seeing a birth up close."

I nodded. "I wasn't expecting so much...mess," I said. "And...I didn't expect that...well, it looked painful."

"It is painful," Rosaleth said. "It's pain and blood and joy and love, all together. Did it frighten you?"

"No," I said after a moment's thought. "I mean, I was pretty focused, and didn't really have time to think about it but...no, I wasn't frightened. Um. Will I ever...be able to do that?"

Rosaleth set down her cloth and hugged me. "Yes, my little Tally, if you want to, when we've finished your changes, you'll be able to be a mother if you want. It's a big decision, though. You won't be able to go dashing around willy nilly when you're responsible for someone else."

"I'm not really dashing around willy nilly right now," I said, then paused. "Were you and Master Valiant planning to go...willy nilly-ing?" I asked her.

She pulled back gently to look me in the eyes. "We'd talked about it," she admitted. "It was part of why I didn't know if I wanted an apprentice. But, witches have responsibilities too, and part of that responsibility is training the next generation."

"I'm sorry," I said, and she hugged me again.

"Don't be sorry, Tally," she said.

"I, for one, expected far less noise. Are all human things so round-about and noisy?" Secret had stayed quiet throughout the birth, and out of the way, lest Gulver or Rosaleth decide to eject her from the proceedings.

"Most are." Rosaleth laughed. "You're a curious one, aren't you, Secret?"

"I like to learn. It's something Tally and I share," Secret said, fondly nuzzling my leg. *"Will you be mating with Simon and—"* Secret cut off as I started coughing, shocked by the question.

"That's not really something it's considered polite to ask," Rosaleth said, a small smile on her face. "Besides, Tally's too young to be considering that just yet."

Gulver knocked softly at the doorjamb.

"I wanted to say thank you, Mistresses." He looked slightly ashamed. "I know we haven't been especially open and friendly to you here, but...thank you." Tears streamed down his grizzled face. "My grandchild might not have been born without your help."

"Your daughter's a healthy young woman, and of good stock," Rosaleth told him kindly. "I'm sure things would have been just fine, but I'm glad we could be here to help."

"I'll tell everyone how gracious you were," he said firmly. "I'll tell them to make you feel welcome here, and that any time you're in town, to be polite and respectful—"

"There's no need," Rosaleth said. She placed a hand on his shoulder. "I have a feeling that people will be respectful and polite without needing to be told. Just tell them to stop keeping their hurts to themselves, and let us help. It's why we're here."

He looked ashamed again. "You knew we were—"

"I apprenticed in a village not too different from Greenwater," Rosaleth said. "It always takes awhile for folks to warm up to a stranger, especially a witch. But someday, someone gets hurt or a midwife is absent, and we do our duty, and then things get smoothed over. It was no harm done, Gulver, so don't worry about it."

What I had taken for bitter disdain for the villagers in Rosaleth's earlier reaction to their shunning us suddenly made sense. She had known that in time we'd be accepted—it would just take longer because of who we were. I felt a new understanding blossoming, and felt foolish that I myself had felt so indifferent to the town that did not want us before tonight.

"Now then," Rosaleth said. "Tally and I should be going—it's growing late, and we must be back to the cottage."

"I'll see you home," Gulver volunteered quickly.

"You have a new grandchild," Rosaleth said. "Go be with your daughter."

"I'll...I'll send my son, then," Gulver said, and Rosaleth nodded reluctantly, seeing that the big man would not be dissuaded from sending an escort with us. His son, also named Gulver, I learned, issued no complaint about accompanying the pair of us witches back to our cottage so late on a wintry night—he, too, was grateful in ways he was not used to expressing. We arrived home a little before midnight, and he gruffly nodded to us and turned to head back, lantern swinging, sending shadows scurrying on the snow.

Simon was asleep on his bedroll on the floor in the cottage already, but Master Valiant had kept the stove going and waited up for us.

"Welcome home," he said.

Solstice

From then on we were, while not exactly popular or frequently visited, at least not outcasts to the same extent that we had been. While our visitors were still primarily those with minor aches and pains—or, more commonly now, those with family members who were sick in bed or injured and couldn't make the trip out to our cottage—we were no longer actively avoided or ostracized by the people of Greenwater.

Of course, the not-infrequent visitors from the village and the winter weather changed the routine around the cottage even further. Valiant and Simon spent their days out hunting, and Rosaleth's lessons, now once again with only me as her student, began to focus on healing and medicine beyond the herbal lore I had already begun to pick up. Rosaleth taught me to discern injuries by examining people using the same magical sense that I used to detect ley lines, and how to subtly shift the weaves that seemed to cover people to help their bodies heal faster.

I also began to learn anatomy from one of the books in the cottage library.

"I know that book is tedious and the writer is a windbag, but you'll learn more from its diagrams than I'd be able to show you without some rather gruesome samples." Rosaleth shrugged. "You'll pick up more as we go."

Simon and Valiant usually came back an hour or so before sunset with the day's hunting—early on this was often very little, but as Simon learned tracking and trapping better, we soon began to have a good supply of meat. Simon would, when the hunting was good enough, set aside a rabbit for Secret, which she appreciated a great deal.

"Your boyfriend is quite considerate," she said. I'd had to explain to her the difference between a boyfriend and a mate after she'd

referred to Simon by the latter term once, leading to both of us nearly choking on our food.

As winter solstice drew nearer, I began considering what gifts to send my friends and family. It was easy enough for Shalla—I knew she loved storybooks, so I asked around town and quickly found a new book for her. For Uncle Grim, I got a nice wood carving of a hound from Gulver the Younger, who I learned had a fondness for whittling.

My fellow apprentices were a little trickier, however. I was fairly certain that Sara would never turn down a good book, but I also knew that Mistress Lirella would have very quickly expanded on whatever books had been left by their cottage's previous inhabitant, and I remembered the heavy satchel of books Sara herself had brought with her from home. Finding a good book, therefore, would be difficult. I resolved to come back to Sara's gift later.

Silke would prove a little easier. In one of the regular mental conversations—we had by now all but forgotten about the fact that we should be telling our respective mistresses that we had discovered this trick—she mentioned being low on several herbs and spices, many of which I knew we had in plentiful supply thanks to the garden and the greenhouse. With approval from Rosaleth I assembled a collection of the spices and herbs Silke had mentioned, and sent them along in neatly labelled jars.

Constance was thorniest of all to find a gift for, not least because we still butted heads often. Ever since she had learned from Silke—who was an incorrigible gossip, as it turned out, though I quickly forgave her—that Simon and I were a couple, Constance's attitude toward me had been pricklier than ever. I had a good idea of the sort of thing Constance would like, but I was not sure if I should even bother with a gift for her at all. In the end, it was Sara who talked me into getting something for her after all.

"She's one of us, even if she is obnoxious more often than not," she said. We were speaking privately, which I did with Sara more often than either Silke or Constance. I had grown to rely on her sensible opinions a great deal. Between her and my fortune cards, there were coming to be very few problems I faced without some insight. *"Just get her something small, so that she doesn't have any-thing to complain about."*

"She'd complain about the sun coming up in the morning," I said. That wasn't quite true, but I was on edge with Constance that day.

Earlier that day she had aimed a barb at me that was relatively minor, but was still under my skin—another Tally the Trickster joke.

"Yes, but you know she'll complain more about you snubbing her than she will if she has to actually look to find something to complain about." Sara put up with my outbursts as she always did—calmly and reasonably. *"She likes things with ravens on them. Probably for the same reason you like things with foxes, really."*

"That's perfect! Thanks, Sara!" I said, suddenly knowing what I would do as a gift for Constance.

Gulver the Younger was surprised to see me back again. "Is there a problem, young miss?" he asked me, obvious concern in his voice, when I came to visit him.

"No problem," I said, then explained what I was looking for.

"Aye, I can make that simple enough," he said, smiling. "I'll have Da bring it up tomorrow with the supplies, all right?" I liked Gulver the Younger. Since I'd helped with the birth of his sister's child, he'd seemed to take me on as an honorary little sister, and would wave to me if he saw me in town. He'd refused payment for the carving I'd got from him for Uncle Grim, and refused payment again for the gift I'd just asked him for—which, sure enough, came the next day with Gulver the Elder. It was a fine carving of a raven, on a leather thong.

"Tell him it's beautiful, and perfect, and thanks!" I told Gulver the Elder, who nodded agreeably.

With that sent off in a carefully wrapped package, I began to focus my efforts on finding suitable gifts for Rosaleth, Valiant, and Simon. Sara's gift still hung over me as well, though I still had no idea where I would find a suitable book. The owner of the small bookstore in town, a kindly elderly gentleman named Artorius, told me he could get me whatever title I needed come springtime, when he would make a trip around the region to replenish his stock, but he had very little on hand that would make a suitable gift for Sara.

For Rosaleth and Valiant, I wanted to get something for each of them that would be symbolic of them together. As the winter had wore on it became even more evident that the two cared about one another a great deal. I wondered, in fact, how I had missed it early on. It wasn't easy to find them something that suited—I had already asked too much of Gulver the Younger, though his whittling would be perfect for one idea I had had. I did not turn to him again, though. One of the other townsfolk Rosaleth and I had helped was a woman named Dari, who was, I was told, something of a silversmith. She'd burned herself rather badly in an accident earlier that winter, and I'd made her a poultice that lessened the pain and soothed the burned flesh. She listened to my idea—matching pendants, bearing an engraving of a sword with a rose entwined around it—thought for awhile, then nodded.

"I can do something like that in time for solstice," she said. "I already have some pendants on hand, so I'll just need to do the engraving work. I'll have old Gulver bring them up your way when they're done—quiet-like." She smiled. "Don't you worry about paying me. You've already done me a good turn, time I return the favor."

I protested, but she would have none of my coin, no matter how I tried to convince her. True to her word, the next time that Gulver the Elder made his visit to the cottage, he surreptitiously slipped me a small package from Dari, containing the pendants.

Gulver's visits were also beginning to bring other solstice gifts, as well. Packages from Silke, Sara, and even Constance came for me, and likewise Rosaleth received gifts from the other witches. We set these aside, of course, to open on the solstice as was proper, and soon had a growing pile of wrapped presents.

For Simon, I decided I would make a gift myself, by hand. I found, among the tomes of arcane knowledge and esoteric subjects, a simple book about knitting and crocheting, including some basic patterns. Despite some early missteps, I was soon making good progress on a scarf for Simon, largely by candlelight in the evenings while I chatted mentally with my friends. It was not beautiful, but it would be functional, and soon it was wrapped up and in the pile of gifts. Simon pretended not to notice, but I could tell he was urgently curious to find out what his gift was.

Which left me, still, struggling to find a good gift for Sara. Simon saw me looking perplexed one evening, as we all sat around the main cottage after dinner.

"What's the matter, Tally?" he asked me.

"I'm trying to figure out what I can do as a gift for my best friend," I admitted.

"Second-best," Secret said. I scowled at her momentarily, but soon relented as she nuzzled against my palm.

"Well, what is she like?" Simon asked.

"She's an apprentice witch, like me, but she really likes books," I said. "Her father was a bookseller, so it's hard to find something she won't already have, and Mistress Lirella also loves books, so it's even harder—"

"I might have something," Simon said. He went to his pack—long since settled into a near-permanent position near where he set out his bedroll every night—and soon returned with an old, worn-looking tome. "When I was younger, I used to read this book all the time. At first, I just looked at the pictures." He set the book down on the table in front of us and opened it to show me. It was a bestiary, old-fashioned, with wood-cut illustrations of creatures most fantastic. Most of the beasts depicted were real, but many others were fanciful creations of whoever had written the book in the first place.

"You could give her this," Simon said.

"I can't! It's yours," I said. "You've brought it with you all this way, after all—"

"It's not very useful," he said. "It's more sentimental value than anything else—and I want you to be able to give your friend something nice. Please, Tally." He shut the book and slid it towards me. "If it will make you feel better about it you can say it's from both of us."

That was what I did in the end—if it had not been to Sara I likely wouldn't have dared, but I knew she would not say anything unkind or gossip about Simon and I, so, just barely in time for the gift to make it for solstice, I sent it off to be delivered to her.

The solstice arrived shortly after, and we all woke up early to observe it. It proved to be another stormy day, with snow falling even more heavily than it already had this winter. Rosaleth was disappointed by that, but said we'd make do in the cottage. I'd barely managed to open the door to my small side-building—Simon and Valiant, fortunately, came with shovels to help dig me out, having seen me struggle from inside the main cottage.

After the small feast, Rosaleth gave the traditional thanks and blessing to the returning sun, and then we settled in for the exchange of gifts. First, we opened the gifts from absent friends.

Silke's gift to me was oddly shaped and somewhat bulky. I opened it to find a hand-made stuffed toy fox, and another bag of mints. *"I love it,"* I said to her enthusiastically, hugging the soft toy.

"Thank you! I worked hard on it! And thank you so much for the

spices, we'd run completely out!" We promised to talk more later—we were all busy with gifts, after all.

"I still smell better," Secret said, sniffing at the toy fox. *"But I can see why you like it."*

Constance's gift was a slim package, and when I opened it, sandwiched between two slim boards of wood, I found a sketch she had done of Secret. I had had no idea that Constance was so talented an artist. I resolved to thank her later, not wanting to risk spoiling my day by talking to her.

"Your friends certainly seem to know what you like," Rosaleth said with a smile. "I'm sure that would look nice in a frame. You could ask Gulver the Younger to help you with that, I bet."

I nodded, and carefully replaced the sheet between the boards, setting it aside. I reached for the package from Shalla and Uncle Grim next. It was practical, as was to be expected from Uncle Grim—a new dress. I had been almost certain it would be, since in his letters he had inquired about my measurements rather awkwardly. Wrapped up inside was a storybook of fairy tales, from Shalla.

Sara's gift to me was large and square, and I could tell immediately that it was a book. Opening it, I was proved correct—it was an encyclopedic tome on the subject of fortune cards, far more in-depth than the primer I had found among the collection in the cottage.

"Where did you find this book?" Sara asked just then, her tone awed. *"This is a very rare volume, Tally—Father had only ever heard of it, and never could find a copy for sale."*

"I have my ways," I said, mysterious and mischievous at the same time. *"This book you sent me is wonderful too,"* I added, changing the subject. *"Thank you!"*

Then it was time for the four of us to exchange our gifts. I handed Rosaleth and Valiant their gifts at the same time.

"You have to open these together," I said.

Rosaleth raised an eyebrow, but they obliged, and their eyes widened almost simultaneously.

"Tally," breathed Rosaleth, "these are beautiful!"

"Miss Tally, this may be the finest gift I've ever received," Valiant said, then prepared to dodge Rosaleth's teasing retaliation—but it didn't come. Rosaleth rushed over and hugged me tightly.

Rosaleth's gift to me came next. It was a wood carving of a fox.

I recognized Gulver the Younger's style.

"You've got quite the collection started, Miss Tally," said Valiant as he passed his gift to me—a fine, heavy winter cloak of black wool lined with fur. "I'm afraid my gift won't expand it, but I hope you'll find it practical." I hugged him by way of thanks—it looked as though it would go quite well with the new dress from Uncle Grim.

I handed my gift to Simon shyly as he handed me his gift. He opened the red scarf I had made and immediately wrapped it around his neck. It suited him perfectly.

"Very stylish," Valiant said, admiringly. "It will add a dash of color to your wardrobe."

"I love it," Simon said simply, and hugged me.

I opened Simon's gift and found a small bracelet of wooden beads on a leather thong. I knew at once that, like my gift for him, it was handmade. I slipped it onto my wrist and hugged him back.

"Thank you, Simon!" I said. It may not have been the most expensive of gifts but I loved it anyway—it was something that he had made just for me, after all.

Valiant's gift for Simon was a new short-sword, similar in style to his own. Simon buckled it around his waist and posed dramatically, and I thought he looked very dashing with his red scarf and new sword. Rosaleth and Valiant just laughed good-naturedly.

"Is all of this gift-giving so important?" Secret asked. *"I did not prepare anything for you, Tally."*

"Our majestic presence is gift enough," Snickers said. He didn't often bother to include anyone other than Rosaleth when he spoke, unless he thought he had a very good bit of clever wit to share. *"And in exchange for that, they do us the kindness of not burdening us with material things. For which I am eternally thankful—I've seen how some witches play dress-up with their familiars."*

"Oh dear," said Secret. *"Yes, I shouldn't want to be made to wear anything silly. Though I do think one of those scarves might be nice."*

"Don't you even think about it!" Snickers said. *"The next thing you know we'll be draped in silly clothes and paraded around for their amusement."*

"I never got the hang of crocheting anyway," Rosaleth said. "You have nothing to worry about, Snickers."

"You say that now," he said, and we all laughed.

The rest of the day passed with us keeping each other company and talking of nothing much. Rosaleth and Valiant made some exchange of gifts in private, but I didn't pry as to what they were. Finally, the snow let up, and Simon helped me shovel out my door again so I could return to my room.

"Happy Solstice, Tally," he said. "May I give you a goodnight kiss?"

I blushed, but nodded. He leaned over and gave me a peck on the cheek, then, blushing furiously himself, bade me good night and hurried back to the main cottage, red scarf blowing in the wind.

This, I decided, had been the best solstice ever.

Blood in the Snow

The next few days were quiet, but not unpleasant. The storm passed with the solstice and left the world soft and white, at least until people started to move around again and started stamping down paths and shovelling great piles of snow out of the way of the day to day operation of the village. Gulver the Elder brought us supplies again a couple of days later, along with some news that was of interest to Valiant.

"Old Filip says he found one of his goats slaughtered," Gulver reported, "and savaged like it were some wild animal, but the tracks didn't look like any wild animal I ever saw."

Valiant's brow furrowed. "Did he try to follow the tracks? Did he disturb the remains?" he asked Gulver.

"No, Old Filip's a canny sort," Gulver said. "Asked me to tell you straightaway, said he'd leave things to a professional. I can bring you to his farm if you like, and he'll show you what he found all nice and untouched."

Valiant nodded. Simon, who had, despite the snow, been assigned to train with his sword in the yard, moved to fetch his rifle, but Valiant raised a hand to forestall him.

"Not just yet, Simon," he said. "Best be sure what we face before we go on the hunt. Stay here, keep practicing. I'll go check out these tracks and then when I return, we'll plan our next move."

Rosaleth emerged from the cottage dressed in her heavy cloak. "Tally," she said, "I'm going to go into town to check on Mother Nash's fever. If I'm right, we're going to see more people coming down with the same thing—while I'm gone I want you to brew up as much as you can of the mixture I showed you the other day. The recipe is on the table if you need it."

"Of course, Rosaleth," I said, pleased to be trusted with something so important.

Gulver, Rosaleth, and Valiant all vanished down the path. Simon sighed.

"I know Master Valiant is right," he said, "but I feel like he doesn't trust me the way Mistress Rosaleth trusts you."

"That's not true, Simon," I said, going over to him and placing a hand on his back. "Your master thinks very highly of you. You saved his life in the fall, remember? And besides, you're coming along well with your swordplay. Otherwise why would he have given you a sword?"

"Ooh," said a voice from behind and above, "little Simon's learning to fight?"

We both whirled, and saw a strange young woman crouched on the roof of the cottage, spear in hand. She looked somehow feral, and it took a moment for it to register—her eyes were feline, and her fingers ended in sharp talons like a cat's claws. When she spoke, she revealed long, sharp incisors.

"And now the dangerous ones are gone, lured away by simple tricks and traps. Your master is so predictable, little Simon!" She laughed and leaped down lightly from the roof, landing before us with her spear held casually, easily, in one hand.

Simon interposed himself between me and the strange girl. "Stay back, Tally," he said. "I'll protect you—"

He was interrupted as, almost with inhuman speed, the girl lashed out with a thrust of her spear. Simon batted it aside with his sword, but the girl just laughed and retreated.

"What happened to you, Magin?" he asked—did he know this girl? "This isn't like you."

"You happened, little Simon! Your grandfather wants you back. He was very angry when you left with your silly master. Very, very angry." Magin circled as she spoke, probing again with her spear— and again Simon batted it aside.

She's playing with him, I realized. I focused, pulling the weave of magic into view, and began working to reinforce Simon's strength and speed, to give him that little bit of extra stamina to help him as she tried to wear him down.

"I don't want to hurt you," Simon was saying, still on the defensive—still keeping himself between Magin and me. Magin swung, and Simon ducked, only to be met by a fierce kick from the feral girl.

"Don't worry," she said, "You won't."

I heard a growling, and realized that Secret was about to spring into the fight. Magin whirled to face my familiar, but Simon took the opportunity to press an attack—faster than Magin was expecting. I called to Secret, "Run! Go fetch Rosaleth and Valiant!"

Magin snarled at me as Secret obeyed and rushed off down the path. "Little witch-girl, thinks she's so clever. They'll never make it back in time!" She began striking at Simon with a flurry of blows, some from the blade of the spear, some from the butt. It was all Simon could do to keep her from gutting him—and even with my help, he wouldn't be able to get inside her superior reach. Worse, he was staying on the defensive, pleading with Magin to come to her senses.

"You're my friend, Magin—why are you doing this?"

"You left, little Simon!" she cried. "You left and you left me to be turned into *this*!" She punctuated her words with a thrust from the spear that broke through Simon's defense, scoring a wound on his side. It wasn't serious, but if she kept going it would be enough to turn the tide well before Valiant and Rosaleth could arrive.

I had to do something. Bolstering Simon's defenses wasn't going to be enough. I stared at Magin, who practically blazed in my second sight—whatever or whoever had made her into this form was extremely powerful, but also completely lacking in subtlety. That was when I saw it—a weave forming a crown around the girl's head, not a part of her, but—

"She's being controlled," I cried. "Keep her back, I'm going to try to undo the spell!"

Simon didn't need to be asked twice. No longer confused by his friend's transformation, no longer needing to find a way to talk her down, he went on the offensive, batting her spear with his short sword, spinning inside her reach, and pushing her back. She raked his back with her claws, sending a spray of bright blood onto the snow. Simon cried out in pain, and I nearly lost my focus—but I wouldn't, couldn't allow this to go on. Picking at the threads of the spell on Magin's mind, I managed to unravel some of it. I could feel it coming loose.

"You left!" Magin shouted as she shoved Simon back. "You left me!" Tears streamed down her face now, and I felt the weave loosen further. I redoubled my efforts, as Simon redoubled his own.

"I had no choice!" Simon said. He threw himself at the girl, tackling her to the ground. She threw him off easily, but looked disoriented when she stood back up, shaking her head in confusion.

'I...I know that," she said. "There's someone in my mind, Simon. Help me!" She clutched at her head, and I felt the last strand of the spell give. Magin collapsed to her knees and sobbed.

Then Valiant and Rosaleth were there. Valiant grabbed Magin's spear from where she had dropped it and threw it away from her, as Rosaleth rushed to Simon's side.

"He's hurt," she said. "It looks like she clawed him—is she venomous?"

Valiant shook his head helplessly. "I don't know," he said. "She's—" He paused, blinking. "Magin?" he asked, shocked.

"She was under a spell," I said quickly. "Someone was controlling her, forcing her to attack Simon. I broke it."

Rosaleth looked at me, a mixture of pride and worry in her face. "Your nose, Tally..."

I put my hand to my face, and it came away wet.

"Oh," I said. Then everything blurred, and I collapsed.

I came to inside the cottage, on the couch. Simon sat nearby, shirt off, with Rosaleth stitching his wounds closed and applying poultice. Magin, the strange feral girl, sat silently, guarded by Valiant, her arms and legs bound by tight leather thongs. She looked miserable, but spoke not at all.

"What happened?" I asked, sitting up with a groan.

"You broke a geas," Rosaleth said. "A strong one, placed by a strong wizard."

"Grandfather," Simon said, and winced as Rosaleth applied salve to the claw wounds on his back.

"Your grandfather is a wizard?" I asked Simon. He nodded, a grim look on his face. "Not a kind one, either. I was to be his apprentice, but I didn't agree with the way he treated people." He glanced over at Magin. "He does...terrible things. Master Valiant found me when I ran away, and took me in. He's been training me ever since."

"I had no idea that he'd been performing this kind of magics on human subjects," Valiant said, looking at Magin as well. "This poor child."

"I'm a monster," Magin said. "Look at me!" She held up her clawed hands. What I had taken outside to be furred gloves was actually fur on her hands and arms, and I could see that there were several other animalistic features that I had missed during the fight—foremost among them being a tail like a cat's.

"Deeds, not form, are what makes a person a monster," Valiant said. "You don't have to be one, Magin."

"Then why am I bound?" she asked, bitterly. "You can't trust me. I wouldn't, either! I tried to kill Simon and his little friend."

"My name is Tally," I said. "That wasn't your fault, though—it was the magic."

"You're bound," said Rosaleth, finishing with Simon and rising to go over to where Magin sat, "because I want to make sure that there are no more traces of geas on you before we go on." She stared hard at the girl, then, after a few moments, nodded to Valiant. "She's clean," she said.

Valiant loosed Magin's bindings, and the girl began to massage her wrists at once.

"What is to become of me?" she asked.

"That depends on you," Rosaleth said. "I'd like to ask you to speak at the Grand Conclave this spring. What's been done to you is forbidden by ancient laws and treaties, and I intend to bring this before them, as well as to bring it before the Wizards Council. In the meantime, you can stay here if you like."

Magin nodded, then took a deep breath. "Tally—she broke part of the spell on me," she said. "Can...the rest of what was done to me, can it be undone?"

"I don't know," Rosaleth said. "It was dangerous for Tally to have done what she did without training, but at the same time, given the strength of the magic involved in your transformation, I strongly suspect no other witch would have tried what she did. You owe her your life."

I started. I hadn't realized that, and yet, it was exactly what I had tried to do—save everyone involved.

"She's a good mistress," Secret said to Magin. *"She lets me have rabbits when her boyfriend brings them back from hunting. Maybe you can get some too."*

"She's—she's not a familiar, and I'm not her mistress," I said. "She's a person."

"She's my friend," said Simon, gingerly shrugging into a shirt. "If you can forgive me for abandoning you and for what happened, that is, Magin, I'd still like to be your friend."

"Me, forgive you?" she said, sniffling again. "This was your grandfather's doing, not yours."

"Then friends it is," I said, offering my hand to the girl. "All of us," I added firmly.

Magin stared at my hand for a few moments, as if expecting something horrible to happen. Then, slowly, hesitantly, she took it.

"Thank you, Tally," she said. "Friends it is."

Magin

Magin was sixteen, it turned out—a few years older than Simon and I. She had been the daughter of a hunter in the tiny village Simon had grown up in, and had known Simon since he was a small child as a result. Simon's grandfather had been enraged when Simon had fled his grasp—he'd hoped to apprentice Simon and shape him into a dark wizard like himself, apparently.

"I didn't want any part of that," Simon said, elaborating on what he had mentioned before. "I found out some of the cruel experiments he was performing on animals, and he always treated everyone else as beneath his notice, or like...bugs. So I left."

"Lord Magnus was furious," Magin said. "He raged for days, and we all tried to keep out of his path, but he knew I was your friend." Simon put a hand on her shoulder as she paused, remembering the horrors that had been inflicted on her.

"You don't have to talk about it if you don't want to," he said. "Not yet, anyway."

Magin nodded. She stared at her furry, clawed hands for a few moments. "I don't remember much of it anyway," she said finally. "Just that I was supposed to find you and make you suffer. I think...I think I was supposed to die, because I know he still wanted you back."

"Well, that didn't happen," Rosaleth said firmly. "And he'll not know his plan failed for some time yet. You'll be safe here, and I mean to see him laid low for what he's done to you." There was ferocity in Rosaleth's tone that I was unused to hearing. I could see, suddenly, the woman who would have joined Valiant and fought against monsters—even monsters in human guises.

"The Wizards Council will not move against him unless their hand is forced," Valiant said. "I have long suspected that many of their number either actively engage in dark magic or would prefer to look the other way rather than risk any restrictions being placed on their own activities."

"That's why we're going to involve the Great Coven," Rosaleth said. "When they hear of this, they'll force the issue."

"Even if it leads to war?" Valiant asked.

"It won't come to that," Rosaleth said. "The wizards want war even less than they want interference. They'll deal with Magnus themselves before they bring it that far."

I moved over and sat next to Simon. He was looking almost as miserable as Magin.

"Are you okay?" I asked quietly, leaning against his shoulder carefully as Rosaleth and Valiant continued to discuss the political implications of what Simon's grandfather had done.

"If I hadn't run away none of this would have happened," he said.

"You can't blame yourself for what other people do," I told him. "Besides, if you hadn't run away, we'd never have met."

He smiled at that. "I suppose that's true. I'm glad I did, that part at least."

Magin looked at us, and a small smile spread across her face. It was a pretty smile, unlike the savage grin she had borne earlier. "You two are a cute match," she said. "I always knew Simon would land a cute girlfriend."

Both of us blushed. Valiant, from behind us, reached out and ruffled Simon's hair fondly—and mine, too.

"They're a couple of peas in a pod, these two," he said.

Rosaleth, though smiling, clapped her hands together in a businesslike manner. "Right," she said. "The three of you kids need rest right now. I am guessing that the mystery of the slaughtered goat can safely be declared solved—though, if you don't mind, Valiant, I'd appreciate if you pay a visit to Old Filip, and lay his fears to rest. Give him some coin for the goat, if you don't mind." I had noticed that we had no lack of money, since most of our needs were taken care of by Gulver's supply runs and the grateful villagers. I wasn't entirely sure, but I guessed our actual income came from selling surplus herbs or medicines. I kept meaning to ask Rosaleth about it, but other subjects were always more pressing.

"I still need to check on Mother Nash. Tally, I mean it—you need to rest. Leave the medicine I asked you to brew to me."

"I can handle it," I said, but I felt another wave of lightheadedness wash over me.

"I'll make sure she rests," Secret said. *"It was frightening to watch you collapse, Tally. I don't want you to do that again."*

I sighed, but had no choice but to agree.

Left to our own devices with orders to rest, we settled in comfortably—Simon and I on the couch, with Magin sitting tailor-fashion on the floor.

"I feel like I should be doing something to help," she said. "I wasn't injured at all. I'm so sorry about...I'm sorry, Simon," she finished lamely.

"You don't have to apologize," he said. "Mistress Rosaleth is good at stitching people back together, and the salve she put on them dulls the pain a lot."

"You've got pretty good," she said. "I'm...a lot faster, and stronger, than I used to be. But you kept up quite well, all things considered."

"That was a surprise to me, too," Simon said. "Tally, were you doing something?"

I nodded. Bad idea—it triggered another wave of lightheadedness.

"I had to do something, and Rosaleth has been teaching me magic to help people's bodies recover faster from being sick. I just took that and...used it a different way, I guess. I should probably mention that to Rosaleth when she gets back." I was definitely seeing better the dangers of using magic I didn't understand.

"You did that and broke the spell on me without knowing exactly how?" Magin said, her expression awed. "Just by instinct?"

I felt an embarrassed flush beginning to creep up my face. "Ah...yes. Mistress Rosaleth picked me as an apprentice partly because she says I'm clever that way. And..." I trailed off. I still didn't know what it meant to *subvert fate*, but I was beginning to suspect it had something to do with the way strange things kept happening to me.

"And?" Magin asked.

"Do you know the fortune cards?" I asked. She nodded, so I continued. "There's a card that I've sort of become associated with, or attached to, or that always seems to signify me somehow when anyone does a reading for me."

"It's the Trickster, isn't it?" Simon guessed. "I've thought about that reading you gave me a lot, and it makes perfect sense that it be you. Besides," he said with a grin, "you love foxes."

"I am very loveable, after all," Secret said without a hint of modesty.

"The Trickster," Magin mused. "I...think I see how that would fit." She cocked her head to one side. "You did a reading for Simon? Could you do one for me?" she asked.

"I'd be happy to," I said, "but I don't think I'm quite up to it at the moment, even if it didn't involve any magic."

She nodded her understanding. "Later, then." We fell into a comfortable silence then, and I dozed off for awhile, leaning against Simon's shoulder.

Rosaleth returning jolted me from my sleep, as a sudden blast of cold air from the door hit my face. Simon and Magin hadn't moved—I had been dimly aware of them speaking softly to one another while I dozed, but it had not interrupted my rest.

"Sorry," said Rosaleth as she noticed my startled and dazed expression. "Mother Nash is feeling better, at least. I'll still want to put together a batch of medicine just in case, but I think it can wait until after dinner."

"Is there anything I can do to help out?" Magin asked. "I feel you've all been so kind to me, and yet I've brought nothing but pain."

"Oh, I'm sure we'll have plenty for you to do soon enough," Rosaleth said. "For now, how about you chop the onions?"

Valiant returned shortly after, as Magin helped Rosaleth prepare dinner. Simon had finally shifted, but only to put his arm around me as I nuzzled against him for warmth.

"Old Filip was pleased to learn that his livestock won't be in any more danger," Valiant said. "He tried to refuse the coin, but I finally convinced him by agreeing to take the goat for meat."

"Just as well," Rosaleth said. "We've another mouth to feed, after all."

"I also set your spear in the shed, for now," Valiant said to Magin. "It's a fine weapon."

"It was my father's," Magin said. "He always boasted of the boars he had slain with it when he was younger."

"Ah," said Valiant. He paused, hesitant. "Simon could use a sparring partner, when he's healed up," he said. "Would you be willing to help out with that? I understand if your answer is no, but from what I saw you're a talented fighter."

"I suppose I could," Magin said, her hair falling in front of her face as she bowed her head. "I'd rather use a staff for sparring, though."

"I'll cut one for you tomorrow, then." Valiant smiled.

Again the routine around the cottage changed. Simon's recovery took a few days, with help from Rosaleth and I, after which he and Magin spent a part of each morning sparring. After a bit of hesitation at first, Magin took to the training quite well, smiling as she tripped Simon up or as he landed a hit with his wooden sword alike. I was glad to see her looking happier.

Rosaleth had been surprised to hear about my bolstering of Simon's physical capabilities, though dismissed my concern that it might be dangerous.

"You're a very intuitive learner, Tally," she said. "That is a fairly advanced application of that kind of magic, and you stumbled across it all on your own. I do want you to try to ask me before you apply this sort of thinking in the future, though—you could stumble onto something that actually does turn out to be dangerous pretty easily."

I thought of the mind-talking and felt guilty—but surely if that were dangerous, we would have known by now. I said nothing, at this point because it felt like I had been silent for so long that admitting I had kept the secret from Rosaleth would feel like a betrayal of trust. I knew that didn't make sense, but it still felt that way.

Rosaleth and I examined Magin together to see if there was anything we could do to reverse her transformation, but Rosaleth finally declared it beyond anything she had seen. "He's tied this in too tight," she said, shaking her head. "If we try to unravel any of it, it'll hurt a lot, and probably won't end prettily. I'm sorry, Magin. We'll ask at the Great Coven, but it may not be possible to undo."

Magin closed her oddly feline eyes tightly to hold back tears. "Thank you for trying," she said.

I put a hand on her shoulder, but couldn't find the words to make it better.

Spring

The days began to grow warmer and longer, little by little, and soon enough the snow was largely melted. I began to feel a sense of sadness, knowing that Valiant had planned to move on after the winter, and Simon with him. With Valiant's relationship with Rosaleth, I knew that the pair of them would be back often, and would likely stay fairly close even while they ranged on their hunts, but I still had grown used to Simon being around, and didn't really want to see him go.

I was secretly pleased, therefore, when Valiant announced that they would stay to see through the spring Great Coven and provide testimony to support Magin. Despite the seriousness of the circumstances, it meant that Simon would still be around, at least a little longer.

"Well, if you're going to be staying, you can help build the expansion," Rosaleth said. She'd spoken to both of the Gulvers about adding a few new buildings to our property—a room like mine for Magin, and another as a guest house, which I suspected strongly was quietly intended to be for Simon. We'd managed all right with the cottage as it was for the winter, and Magin had ended up joining me with a bedroll in my little cabin, but it was definitely more cramped than any of us really wanted. Rosaleth had shown me how to plot the ley lines on a map and we had selected spots for the new cabins that seemed a little bit random to the naked eye, but which would serve to strengthen the nexus, or at least not weaken it.

Gulver the Younger became a regular presence on the grounds as well, as a result, helping lay the foundations and construct the new additions. Simon's sparring with Magin continued in the mornings, but he was also conscripted to assist in laying the stonework—and Magin, once she demonstrated her supernaturally enhanced strength by hefting a stone Simon was struggling with in one hand, also joined in.

My duties in the garden were once again a major part of my daily routine, but Rosaleth's lessons changed yet again now that the weather was nicer.

"It's clear you've mastered the basics of magical weaves and second sight," she said, "so we may as well move into some more advanced magical techniques. You'll need to learn to fly anyway, before the Great Coven begins."

I could barely contain my excitement at this. Ever since Mistress Alina had first mentioned flying, outside the fey woods, I had looked forward to this day. My friends confirmed that they, too, were to begin learning to fly.

"Just think," said Silke, *"We'll be able to visit each other in person soon! I can finally get my fortune read whenever I want!"* She had been eager enough to have me perform a reading for her at the Great Coven, which I had promised her, and now that the opportunity to do so more often was on the table, she was mentioning it every chance she got.

"I'm sure Tally will be happy to read the cards for you, but don't overwhelm her, Silke," Sara said. *"She's no doubt busy enough as it is. Mistress Lirella mentioned that that girl, Magin, is going to cause something of an uproar at the Great Coven, after all."*

"I can't wait to meet her!" Silke said. *"Oh, and of course, Simon too."* I could hear the excitement in her mental voice. I'd worried she would be jealous that I had a boyfriend, since she had seemed to want to meet a cute boy herself, but she had instead been nothing but happy for me.

"I'm amazed Tally has found time to do any learning at all, what with all the danger and excitement she's had these past few months," Constance said. *"Just be sure to remember, Tally, I won't let you hold the rest of us back."*

The conversation didn't go anywhere pleasant after that.

My first flying lesson began with Rosaleth rooting around in the shed.

"I'm sure I saw a spare broom or two in here," she said, rummaging through the various tools. "A rake can work in a pinch, but it's a question of style—ah, here they are." She emerged, holding two brooms. "Now, what can you tell me about these brooms, Tally?"

I immediately looked at them with my second sight.

"They're completely unmagical," I said. "Just normal brooms, aren't they?"

"And slightly musty from spending the winter in the shed. You're right, of course. The brooms aren't magical at all." Rosaleth wrinkled her nose. "In fact, they're a little decrepit. I'll have to get some new ones."

"You said a rake would do. Is there something about the shape that makes our magic work?" I asked.

"Oh, no—in truth, any stick or branch of sufficient size will work. You could even use Magin's spear, if she'd let you. It's just something to use as a focus for the magic, really. Have you ever noticed that your second sight has a blind spot?"

I blinked. I hadn't consciously thought about it, but now that she mentioned it...

"I can't see myself," I said. "That's it, isn't it? We can never do magic on ourselves."

"Right again, Tally! The magic to fly is a simple weave to alter a few things about our own bodies to make them the right weight and buoyant enough to fly. You can use it to make things easier to lift and carry, too. It's considered very rude to do it to another person without their permission, though. Because of the blind spot, a second part needs to be added to the weave, to transfer the properties of the magic to whoever is holding on to the broom."

"Does that mean we can carry other people?" I asked.

"It does, and we'll be doing that to get everyone to the Great Coven. It's a little trickier, because your weave will need to be stronger to hold an extra person without unraveling, but it can be done. Don't worry about it too much right now—even if you can't manage it by the Great Coven, we have enough full fledged witches in the area to get everyone there."

I immediately resolved that I would master the advanced technique needed before the Great Coven, of course—but simply nodded. I was pretty sure Rosaleth expected me to be able to get the hang of it in time.

"Now then," she said. "I'm going to show you what the weave needs to look like." I followed along with her as she assembled the weave around the broom she was holding, slowly so that I could see it. My own weave was clumsy, but it looked like it would hold.

"All right, not bad so far," Rosaleth said, inspecting what I had done. "Now, don't let go of that weave, but try adding this to it." She showed me another weave, a little bit more complex, that fit into the first. I tried to loop it all together as she did, but all I managed to do was knock loose my original weave and the whole thing dissolved.

"That's all right, Tally," Rosaleth said as I groaned in frustration. "I've never seen anyone get this right on their first attempt. Try again."

The second attempt held together, barely.

"Now, you don't actually have to sit on the broom or ride it, but it's a little easier to keep control if you're not worrying as much about holding on at the same time." Rosaleth sat side-saddle on her broom to demonstrate, and I followed suit. I noticed then that Gulver, Simon, Valiant, and Magin had all stopped working to watch the proceedings, and felt a sudden surge of nerves.

"Relax, Tally—your knuckles are white. Better, better. Now, feed the weave some energy from the leylines." She rose up into the air as she matched word to deed, and shortly, I too was airborne.

"I'm doing it," I said in wonderment. "I'm flying!"

Simon and Magin whooped and clapped. Gulver the Younger's eyes widened in awe—he was probably witnessing overt magic for the first time in his life.

Rosaleth guided me further in how to control my height, and how to steer the broom's course. She had me perform a slow circuit of the cottage, staying low in case my weave failed, then we settled back to the ground.

"Good work," she said. "But that's enough for your first time. Don't forget to undo the weave," she added, as I slid off the broom, feeling exultant despite the relatively minor accomplishment. I pulled at it till it unravelled, and handed her back the broom.

"You'll be practicing that every day, so I'm glad you liked it," she said, grinning at my expression of delight.

"*I took four tries to get the weaves to stay together,*" Silke said. "*And then I was too scared to go any higher than two feet off the ground.*"

"*I managed it in three,*" Sara said, "*but Mistress Lirella complimented my precise control of the weaves.*"

"*Hmph.*" Constance, of course, was all attitude, as always. "*I took two, but nobody gets it on their first try. Not even Tally.*"

"*We'll be seeing each other again soon, in person,*" I said, not rising to the bait. "*And we can all show off what we've been doing over the past few months.*" I knew from previous conversations that our mistresses had focused on different areas of study for each of us, and looked forward to sharing our knowledge amongst ourselves.

"It will be good to pick up some new tricks from each other," Constance admitted. Sometimes—not often, but sometimes, she let her evident dislike of me drop and acknowledged my ideas. She'd been nice after solstice—she quite liked the gift I'd sent, and was receptive to my thanks for the drawing of Secret she'd given me. But most of the time, she remained Constance the Cruel, and there was little to be done but roll my eyes and settle in for unpleasant conversation.

"I need to get back to my duties," Sara said, sensing that it was a good time to end our little chat, before Constance got mean again. *"I'll see you all soon."*

We all echoed the sentiment. It wouldn't be long, I hoped—maybe we could even visit home!

Reunion

By the end of the next day I felt more comfortable with assembling the weave on my broom and flying—still slowly—around the grounds. By the end of the week, I felt I had mastered keeping the weave in place, and was soaring higher and faster, though still no farther, per Rosaleth's directions.

"Try to keep close to the cottage," she said. "I'm not sure the village can handle you flying around in plain sight."

"Gulver seemed okay with seeing me fly," I said, a little miffed to be limited to flying around in a small circle.

"Gulver's likely enough to keep his mouth shut about anything he sees up here," Rosaleth said. "He'd be accused of inventing stories at best. It's a lot harder for the village to overlook the supernatural if we rub it in their face at every opportunity."

I could see the wisdom in that, and in reality, flying at all was exciting, even if I wasn't going anywhere.

Simon didn't seem to be too enamoured of the idea of flying, at least, not as something he wanted to try.

"I'm just as happy with my feet on the ground, Tally," he said when I offered to let him fly with me—once Rosaleth had agreed that my weave was solid enough to support two. "I know I'll have to fly with you to the Great Coven in a few more weeks, but in the meantime I'll just enjoy watching you have fun from down here."

"If Simon won't, I wouldn't mind seeing what it's like," Magin said. She seemed far more excited than Simon had. "After all, even if I fall, I can probably land safely."

"If you fall, I fall too," I said. "So let's not think about falling."

"Good point," Magin said.

Magin wrapped her arms around my waist as I sat on the broom, and we lifted gently into the air. I flew, quickly but low, lower than I would have if it were just me—Magin's comment about falling had left me a little nervous.

"Higher!" Magin said, the wind snatching her voice away so that she had to shout to be heard. I hesitated, but Rosaleth had seemed sure that I could manage, so I lifted us up above the treetops. Magin let out a whoop of excitement.

I was distracted, though, by the sight of several unusual shapes wending towards the cottage through the sky. I counted six in total, and realized it was the others, coming to visit!

Letting out a whoop of my own, I took off towards them. As I grew close enough to distinguish them as more than just rough blobs, I took a hand off the broom to give a big wave to my friends. The broom lurched alarmingly, though, and Magin clutched me tighter around the waist, so I quickly returned my hand to the broomstick and focused on keeping us from falling. The others soon converged on my position, and, calling out greetings, we all proceeded back to the cottage, where Rosaleth was waiting, hands on her hips but a grin on her face belying any anger at my sudden departure from the approved airspace.

"Carrying passengers already, I see," Mistress Eve said. "You do like to show off your talent, don't you?" Her fond tone softened the harsh words—she was offering sincere praise.

Constance's face immediately grew stony, however. I sighed.

"There are three non-witches going with us to the Great Coven," I said by way of explanation. "I felt I should do my part to help bring them along."

"Well I still think it's impressive, Tally," Silke said, setting her broomstick to lean against the garden fence and coming over to give me a big hug. She rummaged in her cloak and produced another bag of mints. "I thought you might be running low," she said.

Sara's greeting was not so energetic as Silke's, but I knew it wasn't because of anything other than Sara's own reserved nature. She had grown taller over the past few months, and her sleeves no longer quite covered the dark skin of her wrists—her boots showed more beneath the hem of her dress, as well. She offered me a hand to clasp, and smiled at me as I shook it.

"It's good to see you again," she said. "All of you—though the rest of us have already been through this at least once." I saw she looked more tired than the others, and realized that she would have been flying the furthest of my friends, since Mistress Lirella's cottage was the furthest from Rosaleth's.

"It is good to see all of you," I said. "This is Magin," I added, gesturing to the girl, still standing shyly behind me. Magin nodded her greeting, nervously. She had been accepted readily by Gulver the Younger, but this was a lot more people suddenly around than she had grown accustomed to.

"Magin, this is Constance, Silke, and Sara," I said, indicating each in turn.

"Tally has told us about your circumstances," Constance said to Magin. "I want you to know that we all think that what happened is terrible."

"We're glad Tally was able to help you," Silke said, hugging Magin almost as enthusiastically as she had hugged me. I smiled—I'd forgotten how affectionate the plump girl could be.

"Breaking a geas is complicated and dangerous," Sara said. "I'm not sure if I would have even been able to attempt it."

"She's a good friend," Constance—of all people—said. "You're lucky you met her."

Not sure what to make of this from Constance, especially after her reaction when Mistress Eve had praised my flying, I cleared my throat softly.

"And this," I said, beckoning to Simon, who had approached quietly while we'd been talking, "is Simon. Simon, this is Constance, Sara, and Silke."

"A pleasure to meet all of you," Simon said.

"You're Tally's boyfriend, right?" Silke asked, and I felt the blush immediately rise on my cheeks. Simon, too, blushed at that.

Sara swatted her gently on the arm. "Silke, be more considerate. Still...I can see where the two of you have things in common," she said. She winked at me to let me know she was only teasing.

Constance stepped forward, and I mentally prepared for the worst, but she only said, "Tally has spoken often and highly of you, Simon, and it is nice to finally meet you in person." She curtsied.

"Is something wrong with Constance?" I sent to Sara. The other girl shook her head and shrugged.

"I think Mistress Eve told her to be on her best behaviour," she answered. *"She offered to have her father make me a new dress, since I'm outgrowing mine. I said no thanks—there's a dressmaker in town who we helped out with a fever over the winter who's made one for me, but I keep being too busy to go get the final fitting done. I'm covered where it matters, anyway, so I don't mind."*

I laughed. Sensible, practical Sara, but never fashionable.

Rosaleth and Valiant had been talking to Mistress Eve, Mistress Lirella, and Mistress Alina as I'd been greeting my fellow apprentices and introducing them to my friends. Rosaleth caught my eye, and said, "Why don't you kids take a break and have something to drink inside? Tally, there should be some fresh made lemonade."

It was almost as if Rosaleth had been expecting the company, and left it as a surprise to me. It was exactly like that, really, since she'd prepared more than enough lemonade for everyone. I poured cups for our guests, and then we all sat around the table—which we'd recently replaced with a larger one to accommodate our growing number of residents—and chatted for awhile.

"Mistress Alina's been teaching me about medicines and potions," Silke said. "She showed me how to make that potion of yours, Tally—I'm trying to find a way to make it less smelly without making it less effective." I froze, worried that she would be angry at me for not telling her about my secret, but she winked at me, and I relaxed. "I'll send you and Rosaleth the new recipe if I figure it out, but for now there's always mints. Oh, and you wouldn't believe how much she knows about cooking! I'm learning a lot!"

Sara smiled. "I've been learning a lot about research methods and magic theory," she said. "Mistress Lirella is very keen on building a good foundation before proceeding into the practical. I get the impression that Constance and Tally have had the most general studies so far."

Constance shrugged. "I've been learning a lot," she said. "Medicine, herbalism, magical theory...a little bit of everything. Mistress Eve says I'm a quick study, anyway." She left it at that. I was not going to question her sudden goodwill toward me—though, I did notice that she was wearing the gift I had sent her.

A Reading

Silke could finally no longer hold it in. "So, Tally," she said, "I know you've been studying the fortune cards—since we're all here, how about you do readings for us?"

"I think if she had a tail it would be wagging," Secret said only to me.

"I would like to see you perform a reading, still," Magin said—I had not yet had a good chance to read the cards for her, despite my somewhat woozy promise shortly after I'd broken her geas.

"Mistress Lirella has been encouraging me to be less dismissive of hedge magic and what I would have called superstition," Sara said. "And I never did have my fortune read when the rest of you did."

"All right, all right!" I laughed. "Let me clear the table first—"

"I'll take care of that, Tally!" Silke said. "You do what you need to do to get ready."

Silke—with Simon's assistance—began to clear away the cups I'd poured the lemonade into, and I drew out my fortune cards. I'd taken to carrying them wrapped in a silk scarf, which kept them together. I carefully unknotted the scarf and laid it out—it doubled as a clean surface on which to lay the cards, as well.

"Who gets to go first?" Constance asked, and I realized she was just as eager to have her fortune told, even if it meant that I was the one who would be doing the reading.

"Everyone," I said. "I've been reading about different spreads, and there's one I found that's pretty complicated, but it can be used to perform a reading for an entire group. Since we're all friends, I thought it might be appropriate."

Constance looked as though she wanted to say something, but resisted.

"How does it work?" Silke asked. I responded by passing her

the cards.

"First, we take turns shuffling," I said. Silke began shuffling as I continued the explanation, passing the cards on after a few moments to the next person.

"Then once that's done, I'll lay out the cards—one for each of us, which will represent our pasts." Taking the deck back from Simon, who had shuffled last, I set out six cards in a hexagon pattern. "Next, I'll place one card in each of the four corners—these represent things that are influencing all of us in different ways. Finally, two more cards—one that's for the future, and one that will influence that future. Those go at the center, with the second laid sideways across the first." The pattern I laid out looked a little bit like a starburst with a small cross in the center.

"All right," said Sara. "That makes sense, so far. Which card is turned over first?"

"Any of the six representing us," I said. "We each choose one of them and turn it over, one at a time."

"Ooh, can I go first?" Silke asked, wiggling in her seat in her excitement.

I couldn't help but smile. "Of course," I said, beckoning to the cards. She thought about it for a moment, then chose the closest of the six to herself, and turned it overto reveal The Fountain, depicting a fine fountain, the water coming from a fine statue of a young woman bearing an overflowing cup.

"You are The Fountain," I said—I had been practicing my delivery for an occasion just such as this one, and thought I sounded suitably mysterious and privy to the secrets of the cards. "The Fountain is a source of purity and energy, and when it signifies a person, often represents one who likes to ensure that those around them are comfortable and happy."

"That's definitely Silke, all right," Sara said. "Can we do the rest of this without the spooky voice, though?"

I was crushed.

Sara turned over the next card, opting also for the one closest to her.. It was The Candle, showing a candlestick being held by a young woman in a darkened chamber.

"The Candle," I said in my normal speaking voice, "represents a search, but also a guide on that search. When representing a person, it is usually someone who lights the way for others."

"That's definitely Sara!" Silke said, echoing what Sara had said before. "She's always lighting the search for knowledge!" Sara herself simply inclined her head, not looking displeased.

"I bet I know what my card will be," Magin said, and turned over The Beast. I could tell by her face that it was exactly the card she had expected.

"The Beast...also means someone who has good instincts," I said. I knew what Magin would be thinking, and I didn't want her to feel bad.

"Well, that and..." She trailed off, indicating her tail. "It's fine—I expected it, and it's not actually wrong. The real monster is the one who did this to me, and we're going to make him wish he hadn't done it," she said. I nodded firmly and reached across the table to squeeze her shoulder gently.

"I'll go next," Simon said, and revealed The Huntsman, which pictured a hunter behind a tree, aiming a crossbow at a magnificent white stag—mirroring the art on The Hart from the opposite perspective.

"The Huntsman can represent someone with a clear goal or target in mind," I said, "as well as the more literal reading of, well, you being a hunter of sorts."

Simon nodded, and I had a sudden sense that it was both readings at once that applied.

Constance reached out, but, rather than choosing the card nearest herself as all the others had done, she flipped the one nearest me. It was The Sorceress, the same card that had appeared for her future when we had first had our fortunes read.

"I remember this one," she said, a bit pleased. "A powerful witch, one with mastery and skill."

"Yes," I said, "but don't forget that the card also warns against the danger of pride." I held up my hands when Constance glared at me. "It does!"

"Tally is correct," Sara interjected smoothly. "The card does carry that meaning. I may have been studying them too," she added, a little sheepishly.

I reached for the final unrevealed card for this portion of the reading—The Trickster, of course. Silke clapped in excitement.

"That's you! Tally the Trickster!" she said. Despite everything, I had grown to like the nickname—kind of, anyway.

"Is it just me, or are fortune cards not usually this accurate without some pretty slick sleight of hand?" Magin asked.

"It's not just you," Sara said. "Tally's gifted with a rare talent, apparently, for getting a little more out of the cards than most."

I glanced at Constance, but her face had returned to studious blankness, so I carried on.

"Next, the four cards revealing the influences on us all," I said. First, The Game, depicting a board for a game that resembled chess or checkers, but was identifiably different, in such a way that it was unclear which side was winning and which was losing.

"The Game can represent a situation where there are powers behind the scenes, moving things that affect many. It always has stakes, as well—there is always a winner and a loser."

The next card I revealed was The Will-O-Wisp, showing the mysterious lights leading a small figure into darkened woods. "The Will-O-Wisp is a card representing a dangerous path," I said, "or one that is false. Often there is something that attempts to misguide us or lead us astray."

The third card was The Judge, showing an old man with a gavel evidently handing down a sentence on a sobbing young man. "The Judge is wise and impartial," I said, "but can be cruel in their judgement. It represents justice, but justice without compassion."

"These influences all seem pretty serious," Silke said, sounding dismayed. "I was sort of thinking it would be more like it was last time."

"Last time we had a specific question, or at least, all of you did." Sara was matter-of-fact in her explanation. "This time we're finding out a general future, with the idea that we can be forearmed and forewarned against pitfalls and danger."

"That's true," Silke said. "I hadn't thought of that."

"If I may continue?" I asked, and without waiting turned the fourth and final influence card—The Chasm. It showed a deep rift in the earth, separating two people, one on either side. "The Chasm can mean separation, or something keeping people apart," I said. "It can also indicate a barrier, but not always physical."

"Well," Silke said, "That's pretty grim too. And the last two cards?"

Carefully, I flipped the penultimate card of the spread, representing the future, setting the final card to one side for the moment. The revealed card was The Fey Queen, and it depicted an uncannily accurate representation of the young girl we had met in the fey woods, golden hind and all. I had long ago decided that whoever had made this particular deck had had at least a little magic, or had otherwise somehow encountered the girl-Queen of the Fair Folk in the past.

"The Fey Queen," I said, "represents the influence of the Fair Folk, or a dangerous agreement. She tempts travellers and..." I fell silent as my fellow apprentices all looked suddenly quite uncomfortable—and I couldn't really say I felt any different. This reading, I had intended to be fun and exciting, but all of us remembered our first encounter with the Queen, and none of us clearly relished the thought that she might be involved so prominently in our future.

Simon was silent as well, as I had told him of the meeting with the Queen, but Magin looked a little confused.

"Is...everyone okay?" she asked. "You all look worried."

"We met the Queen once before, in person," Constance said. "It was the kind of encounter that leaves an impression."

"Ah," Magin said. She pointed at the last card. "What about that one?" she asked.

"That one modifies the future," I said, turning it over. It was The Bargain, showing a pair of merchants, shaking hands in agreement—each with his fingers crossed behind his back.

"The Bargain," I said, feeling numb. "An agreement, whether made in good faith or ill."

No one spoke, now. The most dangerous thing anyone could do with the Queen of the Fair Folk would be to strike up a bargain, unless they were very, very confident that there was no way it could be misconstrued. And here I'd just given a reading—a surprisingly accurate reading, as Magin had pointed out, at least for the first half—that suggested that one way or another, it was exactly what was in our future.

"Well," Simon said, breaking the silence. "Damn."

Family

We all agreed that it was not worth us losing any sleep over the results of a vague fortune reading, although all of us were definitely shaken by it. Rosaleth and the others agreed, when we told them about it, that that was probably for the best. Even Mistress Lirella, who as far as I could tell was the most enthusiastic about the fortune cards to begin with, agreed that they could not be treated as a future written in stone.

"Even for a reader as gifted as it sounds like Tally has become, the cards are not reliable, and always carry meanings beyond what can be seen at the time of the reading," Lirella said. "That is why they are not taught as part of the ordinary curriculum for witches. Still, you may wish to remember what you have seen here today— do not let the cards alone dictate your path, but rather let their insight inform your choices."

"What she means," Rosaleth added, "is that most of the time you're not going to be able to make sense of a glimpse of the future until that future has happened, at which point it's too late for the warning to make any kind of difference."

"It's too bad it wasn't a more fun reading," Mistress Alina said. "It's about time for us to get moving, and I would have liked for you girls to have had a good time together before this Great Coven. It promises to be a great deal more unpleasant than most, more's the pity, and we'll be near the center of it all."

"We're going to the Great Coven already?" I asked, surprised. "I didn't think it was for another week and more."

"Well, since you girls are all from the same village, we thought we'd give you a chance to visit with your families first, then head the rest of the way out to the Great Coven grounds to get a good spot. They go quick, after all, with so many witches coming! We'll want to be able to spread the word of what's happened, as well, to as many witches as possible, before the Great Coven proper begins," Mistress Alina said.

"Why did all of us come out to the farthest cottage from home, then, instead of meeting at Mistress Lirella's?" Constance's question seemed sincere enough, and I had to admit I found that a little strange myself.

"There are three people we need to bring with us who aren't witches and can't fly on their own," Mistress Lirella said. "Until we arrived, none of us knew that Tally had progressed far enough to carry a passenger herself, but even with that, Rosaleth would have had to carry a second passenger—far more difficult than just one— or someone would be left behind."

"So, who would like to ride with whom?" Mistress Alina said, her tone cheerful.

In the end, Valiant rode with Rosaleth, obviously, and Simon agreed that he would prefer to ride with me. The thought of his arms around me for the entire journey made my tummy feel warm, but I did my best not to let it show. Magin, it was decided, would ride along with Mistress Eve, who had travelled the shortest distance to reach Rosaleth's cottage and was therefore the freshest among the other witches.

Rosaleth left a note for Gulver the Younger to explain our absence, and I quickly packed a small bag of essentials—the others had already done so back at their cottages, and I had simply not noticed that they were carrying them when they arrived. We ate a quick lunch of sandwiches, provided by Mistress Alina and Silke— delicious, as always—and then set about on our way. As I prepared to take off, Secret leapt onto the back of the broomstick, settling in on the bristles.

"Won't you just fall off back there?" I asked, worried.

"I'll never fall if you're my witch," she said.

"Actually, falling off the broom is impossible," said Sara from nearby, and I saw that indeed, all of the other witches had their familiars with them as well—I had missed it before in my excitement to see my friends. "There's a part of the weave that makes that certain."

"Rosaleth just showed me how to do it," I said. "We haven't gone into too much theory yet, probably because I just keep doing things by instinct."

Sara nodded, smiling. "Don't you worry, Tally. Your weave is strong. You'll have a safe flight."

I could feel some of Simon's tension ease at that.

We took off at a good clip, and I realized quickly as we skirted the edge of the fey woods that we were making incredible time compared to travel on foot, or even in the Witches' Wagon. We were soon passing above Sevenbridge, where Silke, Constance and I had first had our fortunes read, and it was not even mid-afternoon!

We reached Tancred's Ford just before dinnertime, landing just outside of town. I felt a wave of tiredness wash over me as we did.

"We'll camp here for tonight," Mistress Eve said, "and the girls can visit their families. In the morning, we'll come together again and make the rest of the journey."

"Good flying, girls," Mistress Alina said. "Now go on—I'm sure everyone will be happy to see you!"

I invited Simon and Magin to come with me to meet Uncle Grim and Shalla. "I've written to them a lot about both of you," I said, "so it would be nice for them to meet you."

"You're sure?" Magin asked, worried no doubt about her rather unusual appearance.

I hugged her. "Absolutely," I said. "You're my friend, and I want you to meet my family."

Simon, meanwhile, was blushing, and I could tell he was nervous about meeting Uncle Grim.

"HIs name's not actually Grim," I reassured Simon as we walked through town. "It's Graham. When Shalla was little she mispronounced it, and it kind of stuck."

Simon nodded, but didn't look much less nervous.

I found the forge occupied by Uncle Grim and a stranger—a young man I didn't know. From the way he was working the bellows and generally assisting, I guessed he must be a new apprentice. Uncle Grim saw me, and set down what he was working on carefully, giving the young man instructions quietly before hurrying over.

"Tally," he said, " it's good to see you, of course, but you should have sent word!"

"I didn't know until today that we'd be coming," I said, apologetic. "Otherwise I would have. Uncle Grim, these are my friends—Magin, and Simon."

Uncle Grim nodded to Magin politely but turned his full attention to Simon. "This is the boy I've heard so much about, then?" he asked, looking him over. Simon blushed a little and did his best not to fidget.

"What did you tell him about me?" he whispered to me.

"Speak up, lad!" Uncle Grim said in a loud voice, and Simon shot to attention.

"I was asking Tally what she had written about me, sir," he said.

"I like him," Uncle Grim decided. "Honest, and he looks pretty capable."

Magin hid a giggle behind her hand.

"Shalla's inside, cooking dinner," Uncle Grim said. "Tally, why don't you and Magin go inside and let her know we'll have three more tonight, and I'll show your young man around the place."

I nodded, as Simon looked at me with a mixture of panic and relief that he had evidently passed the first test.

"Be nice to him, Uncle Grim," I said.

Shalla was overjoyed to see me—and looked healthier than she had since I could remember. I had been surprised to hear Uncle Grim say she was cooking, but this was even more shocking to me.

"Your medicines have been working very well," she said, with a smile. "This must be Magin? It's wonderful to meet you!" She took Magin's hands in her own. "Tally has told us so much about you— I'm so sorry about what happened, but if there's a way to make it right, Tally will find it. She's very good at that!"

Magin smiled. "Yes, it's thanks to her that I'm even here," she said. "Did she tell you that I owe her my life?"

I hadn't, since I had felt that Magin didn't owe me anything. Shalla shook her head, and smiled again. "She's also very humble. Did I hear Uncle Grim talking to a boy out there? Is that Simon?" she asked.

"Yes," I said. "I think he's giving him some kind of manly speech about dating his niece. I hope he doesn't scare him too much." I had never seen Uncle Grim behave like this before, so I didn't know what to expect.

Shalla just laughed, though. "It was the same when Darin and I started walking out together," she said, blushing. "Darin's his new apprentice—he's very kind and sweet, and—well, you'll meet him properly at dinner. Anyway, when he and I started, Uncle Grim got all noisy and put him through a bit of a grilling—questions about his intentions, that sort of thing. I gather it's some kind of tradition. Your Simon should be fine, if he's half as brave as your letters have said."

"I wouldn't worry, Tally," Magin said, nodding her agreement with my sister. "The men around my village always used to do the same thing, when their daughters were seeing a lad. It's normal."

"And this must be Secret," Shalla said, crouching to let Secret sniff her hand. Secret nuzzled the offered hand, but kept quiet—I got the impression she was trying not to scare my family.

Sure enough, when Simon and Uncle Grim came inside, with Darin close behind, all three were laughing together at some jest Uncle Grim had shared. It was strange to see him so happy, when as long as I could remember he had looked—well, grim. I guessed that Shalla's improving health and my own improved situation had eased the worries that had plagued him all my life before I'd met Rosaleth.

"I hope everyone likes stew," Shalla said. "We'll not have any leftovers tonight, but that's fine, since we'll have good company!"

After dinner, I excused myself to go for a walk around the village. Shalla was in close conversation with Magin, who seemed happy to be talking to another girl close to her own age without having to worry about being treated differently because of her appearance, and Simon had been coaxed into sharing the tale of the wyvern hunt that had injured Valiant before we'd met. Darin and Uncle Grim both seemed quite impressed, which pleased me—I was glad Simon was getting along with them. I wanted to get some fresh air, though, and nobody seemed to mind, so I quietly stepped out and began walking. Secret padded along silently behind me.

The village hadn't changed much, but I felt somehow that it was at the same time completely, and irrevocably altered from how I had left it. I decided that it was me who had changed, and sighed. A group of boys ran past in the twilight, pausing only a moment to glance at me—the same boys who would have thrown insults and sometimes stones at me before I had become a witch. Now I was merely a moment's curiosity for them, a strange girl in black that they didn't recognize.

There too were the familiar shops—Sara's family's bookstore, and Silke's family's bakery. Even the dressmaker's shop felt familiar—though I had never been inside. There on the steps in front, though, sat Constance, her head in her hands.

I approached hesitantly. "Constance?" I asked softly.

She looked up at me, and I could see tears running down her face. "Oh," she said, voice absent of malice. "It's you. Of course it's you."

"What's the matter?" I asked, coming in closer, sitting next to her. "Did something happen to your family?"

She stared at me a moment, then sighed. "No, nothing happened to them in the sense you mean, I think. Mother and father are both fine. They just...aren't living together anymore."

"Oh," I said. "I'm sorry."

"It's not your fault," she said. "You don't have to be sorry. It's not my fault, either, they say, but they weren't like this before I left."

"Oh Constance," I said, "don't blame yourself. You can't."

"Well I do," she snapped, then sighed, the rancor going back out of her. "I can't help how I feel, Tally. I know you and I don't get along, but you're the only one who's likely to understand what I'm going through right now. It must have been worse for you."

I realized she was talking about my parents, and I gently put an arm around her shoulder. "Your parents aren't gone, Constance," I said, speaking slowly and carefully, not wanting to say the wrong thing. "They may not be together anymore but they still love you, right? Your mother loves you, and your father loves you. That's the important thing."

Constance breathed in deeply and let out a slow sigh. "I just wanted to have a nice evening with my family," she said. "But my family isn't a family at all anymore, or at least, that's how it feels. You're right, though—they do still love me." She sniffled, and forced a smile, slightly bitter. "You always manage to be right, you know. It's what's so frustrating about you."

"I just do my best to help where I can," I said.

Behind us, the door opened and Constance's father peered out. "Constance, honey," he said, "I'm so sorry." Spying me, he asked, "Oh—who's your friend?"

"This is Tally," Constance said. "She's the blacksmith's niece."

"Ah, yes," he said. "And wearing the dress Graham had me make for her, I see now. Tally, would you care to join us for dessert?"

"I had better not," I said, standing up and brushing myself off. "I already ate some with my f—with my uncle and sister," I corrected quickly. "But thank you." I put a hand on Constance's shoulder, squeezing gently.

"I'll see you tomorrow," I said. She nodded, and went inside without another word.

Maybe the village had changed, after all.

The Great Henge

The next morning, after bidding my family goodbye again—less tearfully, but no less emotionally, than when I had left to become a witch several months before—we rejoined Rosaleth and the other adults. Constance was already there when Simon, Magin, and I arrived, but Sara and Silke took a little longer to join us—no doubt spending time with their families until the very last minute. Constance was looking a little puffy-eyed, as though she had been crying again, and made a point of not looking at me. I hoped she was all right, but now that we weren't alone, knew she would not want to be seen to be comforted by her rival, so I just let it be.

"Good morning," Rosaleth said around a mouthful of fried egg—from the smell, Mistress Alina had been the one to cook breakfast. "All ready to go for a flight?"

I was glad she hadn't asked how the visit was, with Constance in earshot. I nodded.

"Is it far?" I asked.

"It'll take us most of the morning to get there," Rosaleth estimated. "We should have time for a late lunch, though."

We didn't linger long once everyone had gathered. With the same pairings as yesterday for our passengers, we took flight and headed towards the Great Henge, the site that hosted the Great Coven twice a year, at the spring and autumn equinoxes. The ground below us looked like a scale model made by a very enthusiastic cartographer—the world's best map.

Rosaleth's estimate turned out to be a little bit off, but on the side of caution. We arrived around midday, as the sun was highest in the sky, and the sight was breathtaking. Below us, laid out in concentric circles spanning what must have been a full mile across, was a series of stone circles. Switching to my second sight, I saw the effect they had on the ley lines—a Grand Nexus, shaped and enhanced by the placement of the stones below. The magical essence here was the strongest I'd ever seen, almost incandescent at the center of the circle.

We landed near the outermost ring, inside the circle.

"We'll set our camp up here," Mistress Eve said. "It's far enough out that nobody should complain seriously about our lack of seniority."

"Is that truly something we have to worry about?" Sara asked. "I would have thought that those who wanted to have convenient positions would arrive earliest to ensure their place."

"Seniority is very important to some witches," Mistress Lirella said. "Most value merit and accomplishment over simple age, but few who are chosen to become witches are without either, and so when all else is equal the more senior witch usually claims priority. Our business during this Great Coven should override claims of seniority for this particular site, at least."

"This place is huge," Magin said, awestruck. "How many years did this take to construct?" Then, in a nervous tone of voice, she added, "and just how many people are going to be here that we need to be this far out?"

"It's not so bad as that," Rosaleth said. "The central area is kept clear of camps so that everyone can gather and speak, so only the outer sections are allowed to be used. We're actually going to be close to it all here, just not so close that people get antsy."

"You only answered half of her question," Mistress Alina said, winking at Magin. "We're not sure how long it took to build this place, because it's been here as long as we can remember. It's one of the few Grand Nexus sites that haven't been lost from the old days, when magic was far more common."

"The history of the Great Henge is actually quite fascinating," Mistress Lirella said.

"And you can talk about it after we've made camp," Rosaleth said, nudging Mistress Lirella and grinning.

"You just don't like history," Mistress Lirella said, though she did set to helping raise the tent we would be sleeping in.

"I like history fine," Rosaleth answered, "but the last time you talked about the history of the Great Henge you were still going two hours later."

"I thought it was interesting," Mistress Alina said.

"It was," Mistress Eve cut in, "certainly more interesting than this discussion of whether it was interesting or not."

I glanced at the others. This was the first time we'd seen our mistresses bickering the way we sometimes did. It made me feel a little better about that, actually. Silke was wide-eyed in shock, and Sara was hiding a grin with her hand. Constance, I noted, didn't look like she was paying much attention at all, however. I worried about that, but I didn't know at all how to help her.

Our camp hadn't been set up long before we began seeing other witches come by, some to greet Rosaleth and the others as friends, others to get a look at Magin and a more in-depth explanation of the situation, others still to meet us apprentices. Magin began to look more than a little anxious at all the attention, but Rosaleth made sure not to let anyone get too invasive, and sent her to rest in the tent when she looked overwhelmed. A number of witches looked appraisingly at me when they heard of my part in the whole situation, but only a few came to speak to me rather than see Magin.

"Most impressive for someone your age," one witch said. "I expect you'll go far, young lady."

"You've already come far," Secret said after that witch had left. *"We are nowhere near your den. Humans say strange things."* She was a little bit unnerved in the presence of so many people—she had managed well enough in the villages she'd visited but there we had not had a near-constant stream of strangers stopping to talk. The presence of so many other familiars was also putting her on edge—it was noisy for her both mentally and physically. Rosaleth told me she'd probably get used to it in a day or so, but I still gave Secret a big hug to comfort her every now and then. She would nuzzle my cheek affectionately each time.

Most of the witches just greeted us, introduced themselves— and with the number of people here, I quickly realized I would remember very few of their names—and moved along, though. It seemed as though the early days, before the Great Coven began, were a social gathering, a place for old friends to gather and gossip, and new friendships to be made.

Nor, it turned out, were we the only apprentices. I realized that I'd never really thought about it—but if three or four girls were selected to become witches every year, there would still be plenty of girls near our own age for us to meet. More than that, though, it seemed we weren't the only new apprentices to have been chosen.

The first of the other new apprentices I met was Emerald. She was a tall girl, with freckles and a small brown rat on her shoulder, and she stopped by just after dinnertime. Her mistress had not been part of a group, and she'd been the only girl selected from her village. She'd come looking for us as soon as she'd heard there were other girls here her age.

"Pleased to meet you all," she said, curtsying politely. "Um, I've heard a lot about you since I arrived. Is it true that one of you undid a wizard's geas on your own? A full-fledged wizard?"

I coughed to hide my embarrassment, but Silke was eager to jump in and explain.

"Oh yes," she said, exuberant as ever "Tally did that—without any special training or anything! She just reached in and—yank!—pulled the weave apart! Isn't that amazing?"

Emerald nodded, eyes wide. "We have a lot of wizards out where I live, and I'm scared of them. My mistress says they're powerful on their own, but that we witches are stronger together."

I realized that I'd never given much thought to the difference between a witch and a wizard, certainly not enough to be able to tell who would be more powerful. As far as I had figured, everyone used magic the same way—it hadn't occurred to me that a wizard's methodology might be different.

Fortunately, Sara was there, and she evidently had—or it had been a part of Mistress Lirella's curriculum that was absent from Rosaleth's so far.

"Wizards don't use ley lines the same way we do," Sara said. "We draw from them as the power is needed, but leave the overall flow uninterrupted. It means our power individually can vary depending on where we are. Wizards weave spells into their staves that constantly draw power and store it for later use—they can thereby utilize more power at once than a witch, regardless of location, but they are reliant on their staves to be able to use more than the most basic magic. Additionally, wizards tend towards being very secretive, and witches more towards being cooperative."

"I'm pretty sure we all knew that," Constance said peevishly. I would have objected that I hadn't, but Constance had been growing more and more irritable as the day went on and I didn't much want to trigger an argument, even if it was better than seeing her listless and unresponsive. So I said nothing.

"Sorry, Constance, but I actually hadn't known all of that," Simon said. I nearly cringed, but she just stared at him for a few moments.

"Sorry," she said, looking away finally. "I forgot."

"Um, anyway, I hope we can all be friends," Emerald said. "My mistress usually gives me leave in the evenings—may I come visit again?"

"Sure!" Silke said. "It's always good to have more friends, isn't it?"

The day finally drew to a close, and we all retreated to the tent. Magin was already there, sleeping fitfully. I resolved to try to run interference for her a little more. At least there I felt like I could do something to help. Constance's situation bothered me more than I would have expected even days before, and I could think of nothing at all that I could do to change anything for her. The fortune cards were no help, either—I pulled a single card, focusing on what I could do to help Constance, but it was just The Trickster. I loved the card, but I couldn't see how it would apply in this circumstance. I felt frustratingly helpless, and that, as much as the unfamiliar surroundings and the noise of so many other people, kept me awake long into the night.

The Wizards

Over the next couple days more and more witches arrived, and we fell into a routine—Simon, myself, or both were with Magin at all times, usually joined by Sara or Silke as well. I tried to make sure we stayed near Constance as much as possible too, but she seemed to want to be alone, and that made it difficult, since I wanted to make sure that Magin wasn't left to be poked and prodded at by any witch that felt like examining her. We'd promised her that we'd have the best healers look at the weaves that had transformed her, though, and they arrived on our third day—as did a delegation from the Wizards Council.

There were three of them—two old men and to my surprise, a woman. Each bore a staff positively incandescent with magic when viewed with the second sight, and wore rich robes of a different hue, which I learned later indicated their ranking among wizards. The first old man introduced himself as Horatio. He was clean-shaven but wore large sideburns, and wore pale violet robes. He seemed kindly enough—he was the only one wizard who visibly reacted in shock to what Simon's grandfather had done to Magin.

"I will do all in my power to see that justice is done for this poor child," he declared. Valiant snorted from where he sat nearby—he had made a point of positioning himself in plain view, and was working on maintaining his rifle—or at least, polishing it very visibly.

"Your views on my order are well known, Master Valiant," Horatio said, his tone stiff, "but there are indeed those among us who feel as you do that there should be limits placed on what is permitted. Simply because we are capable of doing something is by no means justification for actually doing so. I am here to see to it that that viewpoint is represented, and have the authority, with my colleagues, to speak on behalf of the whole Wizards Council in pursuit of a satisfactory resolution to this situation."

"A pretty speech," said Valiant. "If you're a man of principle, as you say, then we'll have no problems, Lord Horatio."

"Just Horatio," said the wizard. "I have cast aside the pretence of rank so many of my colleagues cling to."

Valiant regarded him cooly for a few moments, but nodded.

"While still pursuing actual power, of course," said the second wizard, in deep purple robes. He had a long, grey beard and a seemingly perpetual scowl. He had introduced himself as Lord Vincenzo. "Horatio is concerned with appearances, you'll find, but the important thing is that we not be led astray by mere sentiment."

I decided I didn't like him.

"You're talking about a real person," I said. "You're talking about my friend."

He waved a hand at me. "Indeed, and I am not saying that I agree with what was done. In fact, I find it quite abhorrent, but there are those among our order who would not see limitations laid on all for the sins of one. There is punishment to be meted out and justice to be had, but let it be for the one who has sinned, not for all wizards. Our conscience should be enough of a guide to us to prevent such things from occurring—I do not and shall not agree to unreasonable sanctions being placed upon us for the deeds of one man."

"I quite agree," said Valiant, his voice carrying an edge. "But I suspect our definitions of what is unreasonable differ. Tread carefully, Lord Vincenzo, for you stand at the heart of the greatest assembly of witches in the nation, and your position as a devil's advocate may well instigate a war."

Lord Vincenzo's face turned almost as purple as his robe. "Are you threatening me, Master Valiant?"

The third wizard, the woman, spoke then, interjecting coolly. "Lord Vincenzo, calm yourself. Master Valiant was clearly sharing an opinion—he obviously does not and cannot speak on behalf of the Great Coven. He, like us, is a guest at these proceedings, as it was his apprentice who was attacked by the girl under Lord Magnus' geas." She wore robes of a purple so deep as to be nearly black, and had introduced herself as Lady Morgana. She knelt before Magin.

"May I examine you, child? I would see what my colleague has inflicted upon you first-hand. Know that if his villainy can be reversed, I will see to it that it is done."

"I guess," Magin said, a little nervous. I put a hand on her shoulder and squeezed reassuringly. "The witches were going to see as well..."

Lady Morgana shook her head sadly a few moments later. "The weave of Magnus' magic was ever tightly bound. It is beyond my abilities, and I am the foremost healer in all the orders of wizardry. I have come here to represent you, child, and speak out against what has been done to you, that it not be done to any others."

"Ever notice how wizards don't like to talk like normal people?" Valiant observed to no one in particular. Rosaleth snorted but looked at him crossly.

"Your jibe will not incite me, Master Valiant," said Lady Morgana, "as I know the source of your dislike for my order stems not from myself, but from the misdeeds of others. As it happens, I bear no more love for those who would use the gift of magic irresponsibly than you, and despite Lord Vincenzo and his faction, I believe you will find that between myself and Horatio your viewpoint on this matter is in alignment with the Council—though of course we must confer and commune with the larger Council as a whole." She rose, looking tired. "I understand that a mere apprentice was responsible for breaking the geas upon this girl—We would fain meet the child who could so undo the work of such a gifted magus as Lord Magnus."

"I think she is saying she wants to meet you, Tally, but I'm not sure why she didn't just say so," Secret observed. *"Valiant is right, I think. These wizards like to hear themselves talk."*

"That would be me," I said. "I didn't really do anything that special, though. I just picked at a loose thread on the weave until it gave out."

"A loose thread on one of Magnus' weaves?" Lord Vincenzo snorted. "Nonsense. Girl, I've known Magnus for decades, and never has he been so careless as to leave a loose thread. Nay, child, you've a rare gift, and I daresay if you ever feel your talents are not being used to their full potential as a witch, you could have a bright future ahead of you as a member of our order."

"You go too far, Lord Vincenzo," snapped Lady Morgana. "We are not here to steal away apprentices, nor cast aspersions on our sisters in magic. You will apologize at once."

"Forgive my error," Lord Vincenzo said, noticing Rosaleth and Valiant scowling nearby as well. "I mis-spoke. I simply intended to convey my sincere awe at your talent, child."

"Her name is Tally," Magin said. "I think I'm tired now—please, if you're finished, I'd like you to go."

Horatio and Lady Morgana both bowed, while Lord Vincenzo simply drew himself to his full height and followed the others out.

"That was tense," Silke said. "I think that the odds are looking good for us though, aren't they? Two of the three wizards said they were here to support Magin, right?"

Rosaleth sighed. "I wish it were that simple, but if you hadn't picked up on it, the thing about wizards is they love politics, and they love talking. They're experts at saying something that sounds like it means one thing but actually means something else entirely."

"So we won't know how this is going to go until they're ready to announce their decision?" Silke asked, frowning. "Even though two of them were really upset and said that this Lord Magnus did something terrible to poor Magin?"

"That's right," Valiant said. "The most important thing to most wizards is power. Even that fellow Horatio—he's one of the highest ranked wizards around, judging by his robes, so giving up the trappings of his title is a meaningless gesture. He could speak and dozens of lesser-ranked wizards, who still wear their titles proudly, would leap to obey him in the hopes that they'd be able to climb in prestige themselves." He frowned. "He did seem a bit more likeable than most wizards, though, I'll give him that."

"They all seemed to know you, Master Valiant," Simon said. He'd been silent throughout, almost strangely so, given it was his grandfather who was the source of Magin's curse and the subject of discussion.

"Aye, they do," Valiant said. "I was an apprentice to a wizard, when I was your age. It didn't end well—I broke my master's staff in disgust and fury at his abuse of power and privilege. He was one of their Council members. They all know that I'm capable of taking them down a notch or two."

"Couldn't your master just make another staff?" I asked.

"The wizard's staff takes years to create," Valiant said. "They bind all of their spells and power into it, so if it is ever lost, they have to begin again—usually from nothing, unless they had the foresight to prepare a second staff, and doing so would take away from the power they were investing into their primary staff, so that's pretty rare. In my former master's case, he hadn't been prepared, and when I saw him last he was no more than a tattered beggar. Wizards don't make friends easy with other wizards, so everyone else was more than happy to kick him while he was down, where witches would have helped a fallen sister back up."

Rosaleth put an arm around Valiant fondly. "Val's one of the few to ever break his own staff and give up wizardry," she said. "He decided to fight injustice and abuse, and defend those who can't defend themselves instead."

"Simon didn't have a staff, but he walked away from it too," Magin said. "I can see why you'd take him as your apprentice."

"Actually," Valiant said, "speaking of that, I have an offer for you, Magin, that I was planning to save till this was all over—I was hoping that someone would be able to undo the spells laid on you, but if Morgana can't do it I doubt even the finest healers the witches have will be able to. I know you've been put through a lot, but you've got strength and skill, and you understand what the stakes can be. I'd like you to consider joining Simon and I—as a part of our team, you could help us protect others. You don't have to answer now, but I think you'd make a great hunter." He rose, smiling at Magin. "But for now, get some rest—it's going to be a long week, I think."

The Great Coven

Valiant turned out to be correct, of course. More and more witches arrived, until the entire outer circle of the Great Henge was full of campsites. The number of visitors coming to see Magin slowed down somewhat as Rosaleth and the others put out word that she was overwhelmed and not to be pestered. The presence of the three wizards did much to overtake Magin as a topic of curiosity, as well, and I heard that the three of them had no end of curious visitors eager to discuss the case against Lord Magnus, Magin's curse, or even just debate magical theory.

Finally, the Great Coven itself was declared begun, announced by an elderly but dignified witch, whose name was Mother Hesther, her voice amplified with magic to reach everyone. Given the circumstances, the group of us were allowed positions very near the proceedings, however. I was growing used to the stares, though Magin shifted in clear discomfort as the stares locked on her, often accompanied by whispers.

"Sisters!" Mother Hesther began, standing at the center of the great circle of stones. "I welcome all of you to this Great Coven, and bid you good health. As many of you know, we have a matter of grave importance before us, so I will cut directly to the core—A wizard has used magic to transform an innocent girl into a weapon, sent against the apprentice of Master Valiant, the monster hunter, whom most of you know by reputation and by deed. This girl was saved only by the quick thinking and natural talent of an apprentice witch, who was able to disrupt and dispel the geas laid upon her and who I would now call upon for recognition. Tally, please step forward!"

Surprised, I stepped towards the center of the stone circle almost in a daze. No one had prepared me for this, and I felt all eyes upon me as I reached Mother Hesther's side. She laid her gnarled hand on my shoulder, and spoke again.

"Tally has come to us but this past year as an apprentice, and is among the newest of our sisterhood. And yet, already she has demonstrated the will, the power, and most importantly the heart that will set her apart as one of the leaders of the next generation of witches. While Master Valiant's apprentice was under attack, Tally bolstered his strength, but also found a way to avoid any loss of life from this tragic and monstrous attack. It is thanks to her quick thinking and intuitive grasp of magic that both Magin, the girl who was sent as an assassin, and Simon, the boy who was her target, live today. Let us all honor her!"

A cheer arose from the crowd. I felt my cheeks grow hot, and did my best not to bolt for cover and hide somewhere. I wished someone had warned me that this was Mother Hesther's plan— but I could see that Rosaleth, Mistress Eve, and the others had not expected it either. Rosaleth was openly crying tears of delight, and Mistress Eve nodded at me respectfully. Constance stared at me expressionlessly for several moments, then turned her back and began pushing her way back through the crowd. I wanted to go after her, but Mother Hesther's hand was still firmly on my shoulder. I made up my mind to speak to her back at the tent that night, whether or not it would start an argument—I couldn't just leave things the way they were, with Constance so depressed and angry.

Mother Hesther finally raised a hand for silence. It fell slowly, rippling out from the center of the crowd as witches hushed their neighbours or noticed the old woman's pose.

"Tally has brought her friends today—Magin, please come join us, and you as well, young Simon. Many of you have seen firsthand the transformative weaves wrought upon Magin, such that even our most capable healers have admitted that it is beyond them to return her to her previous form. Magin, I am truly sorry that you have borne so much, from your initial transformation to being the focus of so much attention, attention that you clearly do not seek. I say to you, here and now, that this assembly, this Great Coven, shall not disband except to mete out justice and prevent others from sharing your fate. Please, accept from me on behalf of all of us this token, which will grant you the right of sanctuary and aid from any witch so long as you shall live." She reached into a pouch at her side and produced a charm on a leather thong, and draped it around Magin's neck.

"I thank you," Magin said, her voice choked up with emotion. She looked even more overwhelmed than I felt, and I couldn't help but feel sorry for her.

Mother Hesther moved along in the proceedings briskly—she had evidently invited Simon to join us simply to provide Magin and I a little more support, since she did not address him directly as she had Magin and I. For this, he did not look ungrateful. I slipped my hand into his, and he squeezed it reassuringly.

"As is to be expected, as this matter also concerns the Wizards Council, they have sent delegates to discuss this matter before the Great Coven. I present Horatio, Lord Vincenzo, and Lady Morgana, who I have been assured have the authority to speak on behalf of the entire Council to arrive at a resolution to this matter that will be righteous and just. Let us hope that they are wise in their judgement, sisters." Mother Hesther left the threat in the air, implicit.

Lady Morgana rose then, and stepped forward flanked by her colleagues.

"After much debate and discussion, both with our honorable sisters in magic here gathered and our own orders, the Wizards Council wishes to be known the following: Firstly, inasmuch as Lord Magnus has allegedly violated the rights of the girl, Magin, and caused her to be transformed against her will, and secondly, inasmuch as Lord Magnus has allegedly laid upon her a geas to track and kill the boy Simon, apprentice to Master Valiant, and thirdly that these alleged actions have involved witchdom into the affairs of the Council of Wizards, we declare Lord Magnus to be stripped of all rank, responsibility and titles conferred thereby."

I wasn't really sure if I followed through all the fancy speech, but I definitely didn't like the number of 'allegedly' I heard in there, and I could tell by the murmuring from the crowd that I was not alone. But the wizards weren't finished. Lord Vincenzo stepped forward, clearing his throat.

"Inasmuch as the aforementioned deeds of the man Magnus are currently unproven—" Lord Vincenzo had to raise a hand to forestall the rising murmurs, and waited for the shouted objections to die down before continuing, "—in the eyes of the Council of Wizards, the Council does not accept any sanctions or limitations to be placed upon members in good standing—"

Again, he had to wait for the murmurs and objections to die

down before he was able to continue, though this time it took a good deal longer for them to do so. "—to be placed upon members in good standing, with the understanding that further review of this matter is to take place at the next full meeting of the Council of Wizards, where the possibility will be revisited upon full consideration, and not at the dictates of an external body."

Lord Vincenzo was subjected to a jeering chorus of boos from the crowd as he stepped back. Horatio stepped forward and cleared his throat, but waited for the crowd to once again grow silent before he spoke.

"The Council of Wizards does agree, however, that immediate sanction and action shall be placed upon the man Magnus, above and beyond being stripped of rank and title. As he is not a member in good standing of the Council of Wizards, the Council hereby declares Magnus to be anathema. His staff is to be broken, his assets to be seized, his research destroyed that none may reap the benefits of his experimentation in order to repeat his misdeeds. He will then be taken for trial before the Council of Wizards to determine whether his actions warrant further punishment. The Council of Wizards agrees that as the witches have brought this matter before us and as the witches have been placed at risk by this man's actions, the execution of this sentence shall be carried out by a joint task force comprised of members of the Great Coven and the Council of Wizards alike, with special dispensation to include Master Valiant if he so chooses."

This sounded a lot better to me, and the reaction of the crowd was far more positive than it had been for Lord Vincenzo.

"Clever wizards," Secret said from beside me. *"They place the decision that they know will be disliked between the parts of their decision that they know will please, and hope they will be allowed to get away with it."*

I frowned, but she was right. This wasn't a total victory—the wizards were clearly adroit at the game of politics.

Mother Hesther stepped forward and spoke once more. "Sisters, do we accept this judgement upon the wizard, Magnus?"

A resounding roar of approval came from the crowd.

"Then the next task before us, sisters, is to nominate those who will be sent to bring Magnus to justice!"

The deliberations took hours. Simon and Magin and I were allowed to return to our friends, and in the end Rosaleth, Mistress

Eve, Valiant, and several witches I did not know were chosen as the representatives of the Great Coven in the mission to stop Magnus from any further misdeeds. We apprentices would not, it was declared, be joining them for the journey.

"You've been through enough already, Tally, and I definitely don't want to let him anywhere near Magin ever again, even if it's to get justice for what's been done to her," Rosaleth said, gently laying a hand on my shoulder. "And Simon doesn't need to deal with that, either. I'll feel much better knowing you're safe."

"But will you be safe?" I asked. "I know you'll have Valiant and Mistress Eve and the others, and a group of wizards too, but I don't know what I'd do if something happened to you. I don't want to be anyone else's apprentice."

"I'll be fine, Tally," she said, brushing a strand of hair out of my face. My hair had been growing quickly since I'd become a witch and stopped keeping it trimmed short, and I often found it in my eyes now. "You need to watch out for Magin and Simon while I'm gone, okay?"

Mistress Eve interrupted our conversation, looking more concerned than I had ever seen her, save perhaps when the Queen of the Fair Folk had first spoken to Constance in the fey wood. "Have you seen Constance anywhere, Tally?" she asked. "I thought she came back to the tent earlier, but there's no sign of her anywhere."

I felt a sinking feeling in the pit of my stomach. I hadn't noticed that Constance wasn't there when we had returned to the tent, but there was a terrible idea forming in my mind about where she was. Wordlessly, I drew a card from my fortune deck and showed it to Mistress Eve, who went pale as a sheet.

The Fey Queen.

The Search Party

"Now before we start panicking about a fortune card," Rosaleth said, "Let's rule out that she's around somewhere that we haven't looked first, all right?"

Mistress Eve looked at Rosaleth uncomprehendingly for a moment, then nodded. "Of course. You're right, Rosaleth, it's just—with everything going on, if something were to happen—"

"No one is going to let anyone take your apprentice, Evie," Rosaleth said, taking her by the shoulders and looking her in the eye. "We'll find her and everything will be okay."

"Constance?" I sent, worried, and then to Sara and Silke, *"Has either of you seen Constance or heard from her?"*

"I thought she was back in the tent resting, or sulking, or something," Sara said. *"She's been acting strange."*

"She's going through a lot right now," I said. *"Silke, how about you?"*

"Nothing here, either," she said. I sighed.

"She's not answering me, and neither Silke nor Sara say they've seen her either," I said to Rosaleth and Mistress Eve.

"Answering you how?" Rosaleth demanded. "What do you mean?"

"We've sort of been talking through the ley lines," I said, cringing. For a moment, in my concern, I had forgotten that we had never actually mentioned to our mistresses that we had learned how to do so.

"Oh my," Rosaleth said, as Mistress Eve's eyes widened. "How long has that been going on?"

"Sara figured it out the day we called our familiars," I said in a small voice. "We've been keeping in touch with it ever since."

"I wish you had told me, Tally," Rosaleth said. She sighed. "It's certainly not dangerous in and of itself, but anyone who knows your name can listen on the ley lines for messages sent that way and eavesdrop on your every conversation. Most witches don't use it for that reason alone."

"And the Queen knows Tally's name." Mistress Eve moaned. "And if Tally was talking to her friends, the Queen knows their names now, too."

"I didn't know that," I said, panicked now. "None of us did! We meant to mention it, we just kept forgetting, and then we'd just been doing it for so long that it seemed like it was normal—"

"Breathe, Tally!" Rosaleth said. "No one is blaming you. We're worried about Constance but this isn't your fault." She tapped her chin thoughtfully for a moment. "It's sped things up a little bit in the search, at least. All right. So we know none of us has seen her since she left the assembly, but someone else may have. She may still be here, just wandering around."

"Rose, if we can't find her, if I've let her fall into the Queen's hands—" Mistress Eve was panicking again.

"Stop. Everyone stop panicking, please. Tally, I want you to ask around to see if anyone else might have seen her, and don't use that far-speech trick again, all right? Evie, go find Alina and fill her in. She's got a good head on her shoulders. I'm going to see if Valiant knows some tracking trick that might help find her." She didn't sound incredibly hopeful about that last.

I began circulating around the tents nearest to ours, asking if anyone had seen my friend Constance. None of the witches had, though many of them recognized me and offered congratulations, or tried to engage me in conversation—I had to excuse myself as politely as I could in those cases, promising that I would love to talk another time, but right now was just looking for my friend.

It wasn't until I stumbled across Emerald, the other young apprentice I had met on our first day at the Great Henge, that my luck changed.

"Oh, hullo Tally," she said. "I was looking for you. Someone said you were looking for your friend Constance. I saw her earlier."

"You did?" I asked, suddenly hopeful.

"I was kind of hiding back in the camp area because of all the people. Um, I heard that you got sort of honored by everyone, though, which is neat. Congratulations! Anyway, I saw Constance heading towards the tents. She looked like she was crying, so I asked her if she was okay. She said she was just too overwhelmed and was going to go straight home. Um, she said if you came looking for her, not to tell you that, but I think she really probably needs help, right?"

I hugged Emerald, who looked surprised. "She does. Thank you, Emerald!"

"I did good?" she asked.

"You did good!" I said. "I have to go now—I promise I'll see you later. Um, write to me if we don't catch up before the end of the Coven, okay?"

She beamed at me and nodded, and I rushed back to the tent to share the news.

"You're sure she said straight home?" Mistress Eve asked. I nodded.

"That's what Emerald told me. Do you think she meant your cottage?" I asked.

"She might have meant back to her parent's house," Silke offered. I shook my head.

"I've been quiet about this because I thought it should be up to Constance if she talked about it to anyone else, but when we were visiting our families, Constance found out that her parents weren't living together anymore," I said quietly.

"Oh no," Silke said. "That's horrible!"

"No wonder she's been so upset," Sara said.

"You knew?" Mistress Eve seemed surprised. "Of all people, I wouldn't have thought Constance would share with you—she thinks of you as her rival, despite my best efforts to discourage that kind of thinking."

"I sort of stumbled across her while I was having a walk," I said. "We talked about it. I don't think she'd go back there—I think she must have meant the cottage."

Mistress Lirella frowned. "But if she did go straight to the cottage, the most direct route would take her across the fey woods."

Mistress Eve closed her eyes. "And she might not have been in the right state of mind to take that into consideration."

Rosaleth frowned. "All right, so we're back to the point where there's a good chance Tally's fortune cards have the right of it, and that the Queen of the Fair Folk will become involved before the end of this mess. Val says he knows a trick or two to track someone using magic, and he's showing Simon how to do it. Tally, I want you to take Simon and go find Constance."

Mistress Eve looked surprised, as did Mistress Lirella and Mistress Alina.

"She's just an apprentice," Mistress Alina protested. "Surely we can find someone else who can go."

"We could," agreed Rosaleth, "but no one would. Or, if they did, Evie would be declared unfit to keep Constance as an apprentice. Evie and I can't do it, and neither can Valiant, so that leaves the two of you—who also have responsibilities here—or my apprentice."

"If Tally is going, I'm going too," Sara said, standing up and moving beside me. "Constance may be cruel, but she's one of us. Tally may need help in negotiating with the Queen, and I understand the Treaty of Macomber and have read other fey treaties besides."

Mistress Lirella looked at Sara proudly. "I think that will help our chances," she said.

"I'm going too!" Silke said, her voice squeaky with nerves. "Constance is my friend, and, they may need my help!"

Mistress Alina brushed away a tear, but nodded. "I won't stop you from going," she told her apprentice, "but stay dry if it rains, all right?" Silke hugged her mistress tightly.

"If Tally is going into danger, I'm going to be there to protect her," Magin said, sitting up from her bedroll where she had been resting. "Besides, I don't really want to stay here all alone."

"Then it's decided," Rosaleth said. "The five of you—with Simon included—will go and find Constance, and bring her back here safely."

"Well, technically it will be eight," Secret said. *"Nobody ever counts us familiars, but we're not going to let our witches face danger without us."* A chorus of agreement rose from Starry and Pipsie, Sara and Silke's familiars.

"Eight it is," Rosaleth smiled.

We gathered outside the tents once Simon returned. The sky was cloudy and grey, and there were darker clouds on the horizon

"Magic is weird," Simon said to me. "This is going to be tricky, but I think I can do it. I'm not sure I could do half of what you can do, Tally, I'll tell you that right now."

I hugged him. "You can do things I wasn't ever good at, though, so we're even," I said.

Mistress Eve handed a plant to Sara. "If you're our treaty expert," she said, "you'll be the one who's presenting the Queen with the homage."

"Is that a Briseis' Tears plant?" Rosaleth asked suspiciously.

"It is," Mistress Eve answered. "I'd traded for it to make up to you the loss of the last one, actually. I was hoping to surprise you with it when this was over. This is a bit more urgent, though."

Rosaleth sighed theatrically, and stomped away grumbling.

Magin stood nearby, looking a little bit downcast. "If only I had brought my spear," she said, "I would feel a lot better about going into danger, but I didn't think it would be too important."

"I think I may be able to help there," Mistress Alina said. She rummaged in her bag for a moment and produced a small sprig of a plant I couldn't see from where I stood.

"Spearmint," she identified. "You can technically use any plant for this, but I thought the pun would be...well, anyway, watch closely, girls—this weave may come in useful someday for you to know." She began working magic on the sprig of mint, and it grew, lengthening and straightening, until it was roughly the size of Magin's boar spear. A leaf at the end became the blade, and glistened wickedly despite the cloudy sky.

Magin took the spear from Mistress Alina gratefully and, stepping carefully away from everyone to give herself space, spun it around herself in a graceful and deadly pattern.

"This will do," Magin said.

"Spearmint?" Mistress Lirella asked with a pained expression.

"It's a pun, Lirella," Mistress Alina said. "I thought it would be—oh, nevermind."

"If everyone is ready," I said, "I think we'd better get moving before the weather gets worse."

"Bring her back safe," Mistress Eve said to me, as Mistress Lirella and Mistress Alina continued bickering about the pun.

"She will," Rosaleth said, putting an arm around Eve's shoulders. "She's got her friends with her. When did we ever fail when we worked together?"

I didn't wait around to hear more. With Simon and Secret behind me on my broom, I took off, followed by the others, and we headed off towards the dark clouds.

Towards the fey wood.

The Fey Wood

We corrected our path periodically to match the direction Simon indicated that Constance had gone, using whatever weave or trick Valiant had taught him. Despite these minor course corrections, we were still headed directly towards the fey wood. My hope to at least avoid the inclement weather was dashed, as it started raining shortly after we had taken off. Soon enough, we were all soaking wet and wind-whipped, but still we pressed on. When we were directly over the fey woods, however, the storm grew worse, and when thunder rattled the sky around us we had little choice.

"We have to land!" Sara flew close and shouted as loud as she could, but was still hard to make out over the wind and rain. She pointed down to indicate what she was saying. I could see Magin clinging tightly to her, clearly not enjoying this flight nearly so much as she had our first time in the skies.

"I think you're right!" I called back, and we began our descent into the depths of the fey woods. The rain was lighter below the canopy, but it was darker as well, and there was a much more sinister feel to the woods than there had been the first time we had passed through them.

"I don't like this," Silke said, slipping off her broom and looking around the darkened wood. "This feels different. Where are all the pixies and sprites?"

Before any of us could respond, a chilling cry of rage came from nearby, and a band of short, fierce-looking Fair Folk came into view, surrounding us quickly.

"Are they...angry gnomes?" Silke asked, quietly.

"They're redcaps," I said. "They're not like gnomes at all. They like to dye their caps in the blood of their victims."

Simon and Magin both readied their weapons, Simon holding his short-sword low, Magin brandishing the spear Mistress Alina had magically created for her. The redcaps menaced closer, and just as I was preparing for the worst, Sara spoke.

"Stop! Don't harm them," she said to Simon and Magin. "We're still protected under the Treaty of Macomber, unless we violate it by attacking the denizens of this wood."

"But they're clearly about to attack us! We have to be allowed to defend ourselves!" Simon was incredulous.

"There's no provision in the Treaty that says they can't provoke us into an attack," Sara said, "simply that for us to attack them is in violation of the Treaty. If we don't attack them, they can't attack us. Isn't that right?" This last she directed to the largest of the redcaps, who was evidently their leader.

"Fair is fair," he said, as his band continued to threaten and snap with sharp teeth towards us—but Sara was right, they weren't attacking, just menacing. "Ought have known you witches would know the Treaty, but the last one didn't. Still demanded we take her to see the Queen right away when she landed, like some kind of nob."

"Which is not itself outside the rights accorded to a witch under the terms of the Treaty," Sara said. "Though traditionally it is not phrased as a demand."

"Constance is definitely here, then," Silke said. "She's our friend—what happened to her?"

The redcaps laughed nastily. "Oh, you'll see soon enough," their leader said. "The Queen'll want to see you, sure as anything."

"Is she alive? She's not hurt, is she?" Silke looked horrified.

The redcaps were done answering questions, though. Their leader yelled, "To the Queen," a cry which was taken up by his band as they herded us deeper into the forest.

If the first time we had journeyed through the fey wood had been like a dream, accompanied by various and sundry beautiful and laughing Fair Folk, then this journey was a nightmare. The redcaps were soon joined by other dangerous and frightening fey creatures—gremlins, giggling cruelly, hideous horse-like kelpies, giant hairy boggarts darting from tree trunk to tree trunk, always just out of sight save from the corner of the eye. It went on, a dreadful parade of the Fair Folk's meanest and most dangerous creatures, escorting us as though we were prisoners headed for execution, chanting all the while the call of "To the Queen" that the redcaps had begun.

"I thought this place was really pretty when we were here before," Silke said, a glimpse of a hideous spriggan having caused her to turn pale as a sheet. "But now I'm just scared."

"The Fair Folk we saw when we were here the first time belonged to the Seelie Court," I said. "They are...not nice, or safe, but safer and more approachable. These are members of the Unseelie Court."

"We're the ones that go bump in the night," one of the redcaps said, leering at Silke and snapping his horrible teeth. She shuddered, and he laughed cruelly, then took up the chant again.

"Which court is this Queen part of?" Magin asked, her tufted ears twitching in irritation at the cacophony surrounding us.

"Neither—both, really. She's the Queen, of both Seelie and Unseelie. All of the Fair Folk are her subjects."

"I thought the Unseelie were supposed to be mostly dormant this time of the year," Sara said.

"These definitely don't look dormant to me," Silke said.

"On a grand and stormy day like today, we Unseelie come out to play!" a gremlin cackled.

"Did he just rhyme that on purpose?" Simon asked, as irritated by the noise as the rest of us. "Is that a thing that the Fair Folk do?" The gremlin blew a raspberry at him and dashed away.

"Some of them," I said. "They love language, and playing with it. It's what makes bargaining with them so dangerous. They know all the meanings of words and like to throw obscure wordplay with double-meanings and implied clauses that don't actually mean what they sound like."

"The Treaty of Macomber is a good example of that," Sara said, "with the clause about protection being void if the witches or their companions attack—it doesn't prohibit the Fair Folk from provoking an attack or tricking someone into breaking the treaty in order to permit them to freely assault after it's been broken."

"Aye, but you lot are too clever for that," the lead redcap said from nearby. "Blasted witches, always acting like you know everything there is to know. The Queen'll make right of you, mark my words, like she done for the other one, and then there'll be less of you in the world to blather on endlessly about things you don't half understand."

We walked for what felt like hours, until finally, we came upon a clearing that looked somewhat familiar. The chanting of the

Fair Folk intensified, until a sudden clap of thunder silenced them. Seconds later, a bolt of lightning scorched the ground before our eyes, leaving bright afterimages.

The noise resumed, though this time as a susurrating chorus of whispers.

"She comes!"

As with the first time we had met the Queen of the Fair Folk, her arrival was preceded by her champion, riding on his white stag. This time, the stag too was armored, and the champion seemed girded for a pitched battle where last time he had seemed ready for an honorable duel. He bore on his belt a great hunting horn, and on his back, a heavy bow that I knew no human could draw. An arrow fired from that bow would easily pierce the thickest of armor and was always loosed with uncanny precision.

The Queen's Champion was geared up for a Wild Hunt.

I wasn't the only one to notice that.

"The Champion is in his guise as the Huntsman," Sara murmured. "Constance, what have you got us into now?"

The Queen came next, and I was surprised to see that she at least had not donned any more warlike a guise than the first time we had met—the same little girl slipped down off the same golden hind, and walked towards us without fear or hesitation.

Sara stepped forward, and spoke the same formulaic words that her mistress had all those months ago, as was outlined by the treaty.

"We bid you greetings, O gracious rulers of the Fair Folk," she said. "We are witches, travelling through these lands, and in accordance with the Treaty of Macomber we request passage unhindered. We have brought a gift in homage to you—this flowering plant of Briseis' Tears." She held forward the flower, which a gremlin snatched from her and presented to the Queen.

"As lovely as ever," the Queen declared, her voice still beautiful, but now with an added undertone of amusement. "And yet, something about this situation is familiar. Surely you do not think I would already have forgotten my young visitors of last autumn? Have you perhaps given thought to my questions and come to seek the answers?"

"We come seeking our friend," Sara said. "We know that she passed through your woods, though she came without an offering of homage—"

"Oh, the child Constance? But she did offer suitable homage," the Queen said. "Nothing so lovely as your gift, of course, but valuable all the same. Fear not, no harm has come to her."

"We'd like to see her," Sara said. The rest of us, knowing that to speak out of turn could be disastrous, remained silent, but Silke was nodding.

"Of course," the Queen said. "Come, I will take you to her. But we simply must be properly introduced first, of course. Young Tally I already know, of course—and you must be Sara. The nervous one I think would be Silke—so earnest and so eager, it surprises me little that she wears her emotions on her sleeve. The bestial child can only be Magin, accursed victim of the wizards' plot, and the boy must be Simon. Have I guessed correctly?"

"You have," Sara said, trying to hide her dismay. "Clearly you have the advantage here, Your Majesty."

"Perhaps," the Queen of the Fair Folk said. "Perhaps. Come." She turned and began walking deeper into the woods.

Without a choice, we followed.

The Queen

"I mean none of you any harm, of course," the Queen said as she swept along in front of us through the woods. "If that is your fear, then you need not worry. There are other things that I desire more than to place your lives in danger at this time."

"It's so reassuring that she has said she doesn't want to hurt you," Secret said.

"I find it is easier to make a bargain when the other party is at ease," said the Queen, smiling at my familiar. "It makes it far easier to gain their trust than when they feel coerced."

"Are we bargaining, Your Majesty?" Sara asked. The Queen shrugged.

"I should be surprised if not," she said. "After all, you did say you want your friend back. Ah, here she is." The Queen led us to the bole of a great tree, against which leaned Constance, fast asleep, with Lord Ebonfeather nestled by her side. "Perfectly safe, as I said."

Silke moved to Constance's side, pausing to receive a nod from the Queen to grant permission.

"She's asleep," Silke said after a moment. "I don't think I can wake her."

"I should think not," said the Queen. "It would take a very special witch indeed to undo the spell of sleep under which I have placed her, for my magics do not leave a trace, as mortal magic does."

"Why has she been cast into magical sleep?" Sara asked. "You said she offered homage, and was not in violation of the treaty."

"Perhaps I should bargain with you to share answer for answer, truth for truth," the Queen said, covering a yawn with the back of her hand daintily. "That would make this much more interesting— but in fairness, I have enjoyed listening to all of you talking to each other these past seasons so much that I will grant you answers to your questions without a cost. Fair is fair, after all."

All of us tensed at the Queen's casual revelation that she had been listening to us as we had chatted and gossiped and even bickered with each other through the ley lines. I had known since I told Rosaleth about it that there was a possibility, but there was something distinctly unsettling about her simply admitting it openly. Of course, that would be how she knew everyone by name earlier. Thinking about the number of conversations we had had, all of the various topics we had discussed—it was terrifying how much leverage the Queen may have against us if she had been listening the whole time.

"I did not place Constance into sleep against her will," the Queen went on. "Or at least not without her consent. She came to me and offered homage in the form of a drawing she had made—she is quite the artist, though I prefer more natural forms of beauty, of course."

The Queen walked to and fro as she spoke, graceful in her every movement. "But when I gave her freedom to pass, she begged of me a favor. 'Please,' she asked, 'you must have great powers. My family has been torn apart, and my place as the first among my fellows usurped. Can you help restore to me what has been lost?'"

I closed my eyes in resignation. Constance should have known better than to ask that favor of the Queen of the Fair Folk—should have known that it would result in her wish being twisted and granted in a way that benefitted the Queen, and not Constance.

"Since I cannot sway mortal hearts, and since I cannot turn back the clock, I granted her this request in the only way I had remaining unto me. I cast her into everlasting sleep, where she will dwell endlessly with her family and receive the acclaim and recognition of her peers in dreams most pleasant."

"What did you take from her in exchange?" Sara asked. "There must have been a bargain, or you have harmed her in violation of the Treaty of Macomber after all."

"But she is unharmed! She lies before you, granted her very own wish. In what way have I done harm?"

"Then allow us to wake her. Break the spell you have cast on her, and let us hear from her that this is what she wills."

"Pah," the Queen said, waving a hand dismissively. "It is done, if you must see your friend suffer. You mortals have no gratitude for a good turn done from the kindness of my heart—always with you it is bargains. But Fair is fair, and as there was no price asked then I shall not be made to return a payment, so it is only your friend who has lost."

Silke shook Constance, but she showed no sign of waking.

"I still can't wake her," she said, her voice tinged with panic. "The spell is gone, it must be, but—she's not waking."

"There, you see?" said the Queen. "Your friend chooses this outcome. She wills not to awaken, and so does not. You may leave her here or take her if you wish, it is of no interest to me."

"Wait," I said. "You can help us wake her, can't you?"

"It lies within my power," the Queen said, suddenly intent on me. "At least, it lies within my power to grant one of you the ability to cross into her dream and seek to wake her from within. Whether or not you shall succeed, I suspect, depends on whom you choose to be the one to travel across the border of dreams. But will you pay the price for my aid, I wonder? For one of you must give up something dear to them before I will assist with this."

"Will you guarantee the safety of the one who goes in after Constance?" Sara asked.

"I will do nothing to hinder their safe return to the waking realm," said the Queen.

"What did you mean, it depends which one of us goes?"

"Again, I shall consider the entertainment of listening to you sufficient payment for answers rendered," the Queen said, "though that is a currency that shall soon be exhausted. Only one among you may succeed. Only one among you can change this girl's fate."

I knew before anyone spoke.

"It's Tally, isn't it?" Simon was the one to give voice to my suspicion. "She's the one you mean, the Trickster, isn't she?"

"The one who subverts fate," Sara said, eyes widening. "It makes sense."

"It is indeed Tally," the Queen said with a nod. "For she is a Bane of Fate. Hers is the power to change the weave of destiny itself. It is a rare gift, and a dangerous one."

"What does it mean? What is a Bane of Fate?" I asked.

"You hold within you the power to rewrite the destinies written for others in the pages of the Book of Fate, Tally. You have already done so once, when you chose to save Magin from the death that she had been consigned to by the wizard Magnus. You will do so again, and again, and again, for it is your own destiny to do so. But that is all I shall say on the subject today," said the Queen, "for we have another bargain to make at this time. You wish to save your friend, and I will grant you the power to do so, but you must give me something of yours in exchange, Tally Fate-Bane."

I took a deep breath. All eyes were on me, and I knew what I would have to do—I could not turn away from Constance now.

"You said it must be something of value," I said, "and important to me?"

"It must," said the Queen. "To ask less would be unfair."

I reached into the pouch on my hip where I kept my fortune cards and drew them out. I felt a sudden pang—I knew I would miss them, with their wonderful pictures, and especially the picture on the Trickster card, so like Secret. I thrust them towards the Queen.

"I offer these," I said, before I could have second thoughts. "Fortune cards, given to me freely, given now by me freely. They are dear to me, but to rescue Constance, I offer them to you."

"Tally!" said Silke, surprised. Her hand flew to her mouth.

"I accept," said the Queen, ignoring Silke's outburst, and with a gesture she fanned the cards out before her in the air, regarding them with a smile. "A most excellent deck," she commented. "Particularly the Trickster—I see, of course, the reason for your fondness."

"Constance better be grateful," Sara said. "So what happens now?"

"Now, Tally must be put into a deep sleep," said the Queen, "and I will send her dream-self into the dreams of Constance. Once inside, Tally, you must convince Constance that she wants to wake up—if you fail to do so she will sleep forever, as was her fate and will be should it not be rewritten. You must complete this before you awaken at the rise of the sun, Tally—that is how long you will have to convince her."

I nodded, moving towards Constance and laying down in the grass nearby. "What of my friends? I want their safety guaranteed."

"You need not fear, Tally Fate-Bane. They remain under the protection of the Treaty of Macomber, as do you. Close your eyes, now, and sleep."

I felt the magic of the Queen of the Fair Folk wash over me, and hoped with every fiber of my being that I had not just made a terrible mistake.

Constance

It was hard to focus. I couldn't remember what I'd been doing just a few moments before, only that it was important, and that I had to hurry. But it was such a lovely day outside, even if Shalla could only enjoy it for a short while—she needed her bedrest, after all. She was sick, and I was the one who had to take care of her. Something about that bothered me, but I couldn't place my finger on it. It wasn't that I minded being Shalla's caretaker, even though it meant I couldn't go out to the Choosing with all the other girls, and have my opportunity to become a witch's apprentice. I was happy here, and would never want to leave.

I thought about that while I mixed medicine for Shalla. I still knew there was something wrong, something that I couldn't quite remember, but I was a practiced herbalist now, thanks to...thanks to all the time I spent making medicine for Shalla, I guessed. I brought out the tea for her.

"Thank you, Tally," she said. "You're a wonderful sister, to look after me so. I know you wanted to be a witch, but it's better this way, don't you think?"

"This is wrong," I said. I didn't know how, but I knew there was something out of place here. Then I realized. I hadn't been Shalla's sister, not until I met Rosaleth, not until I became a witch's apprentice.

"Tally?" Shalla asked, but I ignored her—as painful as it was to do, I remembered now that I had entered into Constance's dream, to rescue her from eternal sleep. Shalla was a part of that dream.

"I have to go," I said. "I have to find the Choosing." I began to run, heading away from Shalla in the direction I knew would bring me towards the spot the Witches' Wagon had been parked, that day last autumn, but I felt strangely sluggish, as though running through molasses. I focused my will, and shouted in frustration.

And the scenery shifted around me, sliding rapidly—and I was there. Constance was the first chosen, of course, smiling beside Mistress Eve. Mistress Alina and Mistress Lirella were also standing there, but strangely placid, as though they did not actually care about choosing their apprentices. Rosaleth was nowhere in sight.

"Constance!" I said. "Constance, it's me, Tally! You have to—"

"You're not supposed to be here," Constance said, perplexed. "You're supposed to be with your sister. That's how this goes. I remember it clearly, that's why you're not chosen."

"Listen to me, Constance," I pleaded. "This isn't real!"

"That would explain why you're here and not with your sister," Constance said. "But you still shouldn't be here, Tally." She turned away from me, and the scene of the Choosing melted away, forgotten. "You're not supposed to be here," she repeated.

I grabbed her by the shoulders. "Constance, listen to me. This is all a dream. At the real Choosing, you're right—I wasn't there, I was in the wagon, stealing herbs." I hadn't ever told my friends that part, that Rosaleth had caught me red-handed, but I no longer cared.

"Then why are you here now?" Constance asked, frowning. "How does a thief become a witch's apprentice, Tally? What right do you have to call yourself my peer?"

This wasn't working. I tried another approach. "Constance, do you remember that day? Do you remember who else was chosen?"

"I think so." She frowned. "Sara the bookseller's daughter, and Silke, the baker's daughter. They're both clever, but not so clever as I am."

"If this is the Choosing, then, how do you already know who was Chosen?"

Constance's frown deepened. "I don't know," she said finally. "But I do know it. And you—you were chosen. The fourth of three. A thief, who wasn't even at the Choosing proper. You should never have been picked, but you were."

"Yes, I was, Constance, and we're apprentices together. Do you remember now?"

"I remember...you getting the credit for something...something important. Something that could have been any of us, but it was you, by pure luck. Everything comes together for you, Tally, and everything falls apart for me. It's not fair!" Her voice rose to a shriek with this last declaration, and she turned again and ran from me—but the first step was enough, in the dream, to take her out of my reach again.

I found myself again with my family, eating dinner. Simon and Magin were there, too—just as they had been that night when we had returned home to visit. I had no difficulty remembering what I had to do this time—Uncle Grim called out my name as I rose, leaving the plate of food half-finished, and Simon looked confused as I brushed past him to the door.

"Nobody in this world makes sense," Secret observed, padding along beside me as I rushed towards Constance's home. *"I couldn't even find you at first."*

"Secret!" I said, surprised. "I didn't think you'd be in here with me. I am glad of the company, though."

"Lord Ebonfeather is here too, but he says Constance hasn't been listening to him at all either. He was glad enough when I told him you were here." As Secret spoke, a dark feathered form flew down and landed on my shoulder.

"If anyone can get through to Lady Constance, I expect it will be you, Tally," he said in his sonorous voice. *"I hope, anyway,"* he amended, sounding almost childlike in his concern.

"Don't worry, Lord Ebonfeather," I said. "I'm here to get her out of this place." This time, as I ran, the streets didn't fight me, and I was soon outside Constance's home. While Constance had been sitting on the steps alone when I had arrived in the real world, they were empty here in the dream.

"She is still inside, with her parents," Lord Ebonfeather said. *"This day was so hard for her, I can't comprehend why she chooses to relive it endlessly."*

"She's making a happy world for herself," I said, thinking. "You said she wasn't listening to you—You tried to get her attention, right? I'm betting by rapping on the window with your beak."

"I never 'rap' on windows, as you so uncouthly put it. I knocked like a civilized person." Lord Ebonfeather preened for a moment. *"But yes, that's basically what I tried. She ignored me!"* He sounded hurt by that—I knew that Constance spoiled Lord Ebonfeather at every opportunity she got, so being ignored must have hurt his feelings a great deal.

"How cruel!" Secret said, and I realized that Constance wasn't alone in spoiling her familiar. We were more alike than either she or I had ever cared to admit.

But that wasn't helping me solve this problem. If Lord Ebon-feather had already tried knocking, it stood to reason that I would get no further with the same tactic. This called for more dras-tic measures. Glancing around, I found a suitably large rock, and hefted it in my hand.

"What are you doing, Tally?" Lord Ebonfeather asked, alarmed. By way of an answer, I shifted my weight and hurled the rock straight through the window, shattering the glass. I heard a cry within, and moments later Constance erupted out the door, furious.

"Why won't you just leave me alone?" she demanded. "All I wanted was a nice dinner with my family! Your family is happy, why do you want to make mine miserable?"

"I don't, Constance, I truly don't, but this isn't real and you have to see that!"

"Why?" she asked. "Why must I see that? Why do you keep insisting that this isn't real, Tally? So that you can hold it over me how much better you are, how much happier you are?"

"Because none of this, except you and me and our familiars, is real, Constance! It's all a dream you're having!"

She clutched her head and moaned. "I don't care," she said, "I don't care at all if it's real! I have a happy family here, a family that loves me, and I was supposed to be free of you always trying to one-up me, but here you are! You're ruining everything, like you always have!"

"Your family does love you, Constance," I said. "They're not together anymore, but that doesn't mean they don't love you—just like I told you that day. Do you remember?"

The scene dissolved again, and it was just the two of us and our familiars, standing in a grey nothingness.

"I do remember," she said. "Damn you, but I remember. Why, Tally?"

"Because we're worried about you, Constance." I looked her straight in the eye as I spoke. "Your friends are worried about you. Everyone came to the fey wood after you—Sara, Silke, Magin, Simon, and I, we all came to find you and bring you back to Mistress Eve."

"Friends," Constance said, then shook her head. "Why would we be friends, Tally? I've been nothing but cruel to you, and I know you've been calling me Constance the Cruel behind my back. The Queen told me. The Queen..." She trailed off, then narrowed her eyes.

"The Queen put me into a slumber," she said. "I asked her to fix things, and she put me to sleep. And...you? You came for me?"

"Yes," I said, relieved that she finally seemed to be grasping the situation. "We all came. Mistress Eve was beside herself with worry—she couldn't come herself, and she couldn't ask anyone else, because she was terrified of losing you, Constance. You're not alone!"

Constance looked at me, tears in her eyes. "But I've been so cruel," she repeated. "At first I didn't know you, and thought you were just some upstart who thought she was so special, but later I just didn't know how to apologize or start over, so I just kept going. Why would you risk everything and make a bargain with the Queen for me after that?"

"Because we're friends," I said. "Rosaleth and Mistress Eve argued over whether Rosaleth should take me as her apprentice, and they're still friends. Mistress Lirella and Rosaleth bickered while we were setting up camp, do you remember?"

Constance nodded, snorting a laugh through her tears. "I do remember," she said.

"Mistress Lirella and Mistress Alina even bickered while we were setting out to come bring you back," I said. "And our mistresses are friends. And more than that, they're like a second family to us. Right?"

"They are," Constance admitted. "What did they bicker about?"

I thought about trying to explain the pun, then shook my head. "I'll have to explain later," I said, "it's too complicated. We both need to get out of here before it's too late."

"How do we do that?" Constance asked, no longer crying.

"We wake up," I said. She took my hand, and together, we woke up.

Return

I awoke to a chorus of happy cries and hugs, as everyone rushed to make Constance feel welcome and celebrate that we had come back. The pre-dawn light made the clearing we were in seem magical and beautiful—much closer to the way I remembered the fey woods from my first visit than they had been throughout the menacing return trip.

"You were successful, Tally Fate-Bane, as I knew you would be," said the Queen quietly while the others were busy, all talking to Constance at once.

"I have a question for you," I said, standing up.

"I may choose to answer it," said the Queen with a small smile. "But I suspect I know what you will ask. If I knew you would succeed, why go to all the effort in the first place?"

"It just doesn't fit," I said. "You seemed to expect everything that happened tonight, but—was it all just to get my fortune cards?"

A sadness crossed the Queen's face for a moment, and she shook her head. "Nay, Tally Fate-Bane. It did not matter what sacrifice you made to me, only that you chose to make one. My reasons are my own, and I think I shall not reveal them today—but know that this shall not be the last time that you and I meet." She reached out and brushed my cheek softly. "You have a power not often seen in this world. Use it wisely, and you will be remembered as one of the greatest witches in history. I would not suggest you use it foolishly. But mortals are often fickle."

"We feel the same about your people," I said. "I wish we understood each other better."

"That, I fear, even you cannot bring about, Tally Fate-Bane, for we are as different as night and day. I will leave you now. You are free to go when you wish, but do not linger overlong in these woods—they are dangerous for mortals, even those with my protection."

"We won't stay long," I promised. "Until we meet again." I wasn't sure why I said that rather than farewell, but I believed the Queen when she said this would not be our last meeting. Somehow, I didn't find that frightening as I would have before—it was instead oddly comforting.

"Tally," Constance said behind me. I turned, and she regarded me seriously.

"Constance," I said.

"They told me what you gave up to save me." Constance said.

"I loved those cards," I admitted. "But you're my friend, and in the end, they were just..."

"Thank you, Tally," she said, and hugged me suddenly.

"Hey now," I said, embarrassed by her display—everyone else was watching. But they were all smiling, and I supposed that they'd been busy hugging while I had talked to the Queen.

"Friends?" Constance said when she withdrew from the hug.

"Friends," I confirmed. "But don't go slowing down just because we're friends—it's good to have a rival, too." I grinned at her, and she grinned back. Soon, we were both laughing.

"I don't quite understand what was so funny about that," Secret said, *"But I am certainly glad that the two of you are so happy."*

"We're all happy," Simon said, scratching Secret behind the ears. "Friendship does that."

We flew out of the fey woods into a beautiful morning. The storm had cleared completely, and there was hardly a cloud in the sky. I'd planned for us to return straight to the Great Henge without delay, but the morning was so beautiful and our spirits so high that we spent a little bit of time just enjoying ourselves in flight—chasing each other, swooping around, that sort of thing. Eventually, we did make it back to the Great Henge, where we found things in much the same state as we had left them, save that Mistress Eve, Rosaleth, Valiant and the others sent to enforce the sentence against Simon's grandfather had not yet returned.

Mistress Alina hugged us all and gave us pastries in celebration of our return. Mistress Lirella looked relieved as well, but was far more reserved in her response, simply nodding approval. Both of them demanded a full recounting of what had happened, and were ultimately pleased at how we'd handled ourselves.

"Well done, all of you. Few witches your age would have done so well alone in the fey woods," Mistress Lirella said, "let alone bargaining with the Queen."

I asked them, quietly, if they had ever heard of a Fate-Bane. They shook their heads.

"You do have an affinity for certain applications of magic," Mistress Lirella mused, "and a tendency towards involvement in matters that would give other apprentices, or even full-fledged witches, pause. It would also explain your uncanny accuracy when using the fortune cards—a pity that you no longer have your deck, as I would have liked to examine the cards both alone and while you were using them—"

"The poor girl's not an experimental subject, Lirella," Mistress Alina said, but softened her words with a fond smile. "She's definitely interesting, though, I'll agree to that." She tousled my hair fondly.

Rosaleth and the rest returned that evening. Valiant's arm was in a sling, but otherwise everyone seemed unharmed. They didn't come straight back to the tent, as they were first required to report to the leaders of the Great Coven and the Council representatives. When they did return, there was another round of hugging, and Mistress Eve even cried when she saw Constance safe.

We had to repeat our story in full before they were satisfied, though I burned with curiosity as to the outcome of their mission and how Valiant had come to be injured. Their reactions were largely the same as Mistress Lirella's and Mistress Alina's had been.

"Fate-Bane? That's certainly ominous-sounding." Rosaleth tousled my hair—I was getting a little bit tired of that today, but under the circumstances, said nothing. "I preferred Trickster, I think. It goes without saying that you shouldn't rush to meet the Queen again any time soon, of course. You did good, little one."

"But what about your mission?" I finally said, unable to contain my curiosity. "What happened to Valiant's arm?"

The three of them—Rosaleth, Valiant, and Mistress Eve—glanced at each other. Rosaleth sighed.

"We arrived quickly enough to catch Magnus unawares, or so we thought," Rosaleth said. "He hadn't fled, anyway. He threw a spell at me, and Valiant knocked me out of the way."

"Landed badly," Valiant said, looking embarrassed. "Broke my arm."

They both paused, and Mistress Eve took up the narrative.

"Magnus didn't have time for another spell, before we were upon him. One of the wizards, Ferrus I think, disarmed him, and we surrounded him so he couldn't escape. His staff was broken, and his research destroyed."

"We blasted his tower to rubble," Rosaleth said with some satisfaction. "The wizards took him into custody to stand further trial before their council."

"And somehow lost him," Valiant said, his voice full of disgust. "He had help. I couldn't track him, even with all of my skills and tricks."

Simon looked alarmed. "He's still out there?" he demanded. Magin, too, looked distraught, and I put an arm around her comfortingly.

"He is," Valiant nodded, "but without his staff and notes, he's much diminished. I don't like it any more than you do, especially since he clearly had help, but don't worry. He'll be found, and brought to justice, if I have to do it myself."

"You're not going anywhere until your arm is healed up," Rosaleth said. "That was a bad break."

Valiant protested...but not very hard.

A day or two later, we bid our farewells to the new faces we had met at the Great Coven. I promised to write to Emerald and reminded her to write to me as well. In fact, we had all promised to write to each other, now that we knew the dangers of the magical speech we'd been using to communicate all this time. Thankfully, now that we could fly, my friends and I could also visit each other much more readily than we could before. We decided to take the trip home in a single flight, rather than break it into a journey of two legs as we had on the way out—we were setting off much earlier in the day, after all.

Sara left us first, of course, since the cottage she shared with Mistress Lirella was the first along our route. Then Silke and Mistress Alina were next, and then Constance, who waved goodbye to me with more sincerity and enthusiasm than I could remember her ever showing me before.

"Take care!" I called. She nodded, smiling broadly.

Mistress Eve continued with us, though, carrying Magin on her broom, so that neither Rosaleth nor I would need to carry two passengers. It was possible to do so, but very tiring, and since we had the farthest to go, she had volunteered to help us out. Besides,

I had a feeling she felt she owed me. I would never call on that debt, of course, since it had been to help my friend that I had gone into the fey woods, but I knew that Mistress Eve would always hold me in high esteem, and that alone was a good feeling.

Gulver the Younger had been busy, it seemed—the extra buildings had been completed in our absence, and the garden carefully weeded and tended. Having arrived in the early evening, we offered Mistress Eve dinner, but she declined.

"I should go and make sure that Constance doesn't feel alone," she said. "I don't want to let her down."

"Tell her that if she ever needs to talk, she knows where she can find me," I said.

"I think she already knows that," Mistress Eve said with a smile, "but I'll let her know." She reached out as though to tousle my hair, but, seeing me cringe in anticipation, shifted to offer me her hand. I shook it.

"You did good, Tally," she said. "I was mistaken when I doubted your suitability as a witch." She bid her farewells to Rosaleth and Valiant, and was off again.

Things fell back into a regular routine. Valiant, with his broken arm, directed Simon and Magin in their daily training, as Magin had accepted his offer, and would be joining Simon as an apprentice. She seemed to have come to terms with her new form, at least admitting that it had certain advantages, and that it wasn't all bad since she'd made some good friends. I, of course, returned to gardening and studying, though I set aside my study of the fortune cards in favor of learning a bit more magical theory. Little enough purpose now to me learning any more about the cards, after all.

Then, about a month after the Great Coven, a package came for me, brought to the cottage by Gulver the Elder on one of his supply runs. It was from Constance—I was a little surprised that she hadn't delivered it in person, since she had been out the day with Mistress Eve to finally bring Rosaleth a Briseis' Tears plant. Curious, I tore open the package. Inside, I found a letter, and a smaller package, this one wrapped in a silk scarf.

The letter was short.

Tally, it read, *I didn't want to bring you this in person because I thought I'd get too emotional. I'm so grateful that you're my friend. I know giving up your cards was hard for you, and that you did it to rescue me, so I've been working hard on these. They're not as good as the ones you had, I think, but Mistress Eve says that a deck made special for someone is actually better. So I hope you like them.*

Your friend, Constance.

P.S. I'm making a deck for everyone else, too. Silke will be so happy!

I set the letter aside, and carefully unwrapped the small bundle. Sure enough, inside was a fortune deck—hand illustrated by Constance. I could tell she had put a lot of effort into it, and while some of the cards were different from the illustrations I was used to, that was to be expected between different decks. The cards were beautiful, and I caught my breath when I found the card for The Trickster. It was an illustration of a fox, of course, but it was obviously Secret. In the sky above where she sat, a raven flew. It was a small detail, but it brought tears to my eyes.

It was perfect.

Made in the USA
Columbia, SC
30 November 2017